More Praise for Jon Hassler

"Jon Hassler's Staggerford, Minnesota, is somewhere north of Garrison Keillor's Lake Wobegon, and isn't far from Sinclair Lewis's Gopher Prairie . . . The cast of characters Jon Hassler has created over the years is the reason his novels have a quiet legion of devoted readers." —*Chicago Tribune*

"Ever since his remarkable first novel, *Staggerford*, [Hassler] has moved surely forward in the perfection of his art. His prose is flawless, his characters are decent, believable people about whom you care immensely, his stories are strong. He writes about what he knows so that we may know it too and find therein the power of understanding." —*The Cleveland Plain Dealer*

"Staggerford is an appealing, inviting place. Hassler's portrait of small-town life is deeply affectionate and gently humorous. His many devoted readers will welcome this chance to revisit Staggerford and be reassured that whatever new terror and turmoil is reported on today's front page, in Staggerford, at least, old-fashioned virtues endure and the bonds of small community remain strong." —*Milwaukee Journal Sentinel*

"The popularity of Hassler's series is due to his skill in depicting, with warmth and insight, the quaint shades and nuances of rural life." —*Publishers Weekly*

JON HASSLER is the author of eleven novels, most recently *The Staggerford Flood* (available from Plume), two short-story collections, and two works of nonfiction. He is Regent's professor emeritus at St. John's University in Minnesota, and divides his time between Minneapolis, Minnesota, and Melbourne Beach, Florida.

OTHER WORKS BY
JON HASSLER

FICTION

Staggerford

Simon's Night

The Love Hunter

A Green Journey

Grand Opening

North of Hope

Dear James

Rookery Blues

The Dean's List

Keepsakes and Other Stories

Rufus at the Door and Other Stories

The Staggerford Flood

FOR YOUNG ADULTS

Four Miles to Pinecone

Jemmy

NONFICTION

My Staggerford Journal

Good People . . . from an Author's Life

THE
Staggerford
Murders

THE
Life and Death of
Nancy Clancy's
Nephew

JON HASSLER

A PLUME BOOK

PLUME
Published by the Penguin Group
Penguin Group (USA) Inc., 375 Hudson Street, New York, New York 10014, U.S.A.
Penguin Books Ltd, 80 Strand, London WC2R 0RL, England
Penguin Books Australia Ltd, 250 Camberwell Road,Camberwell, Victoria 3124, Australia
Penguin Books Canada Ltd, 10 Alcorn Avenue,Toronto, Ontario, Canada M4V 3B2
Penguin Books India (P) Ltd, 11 Community Centre, Panchsheel Park,
New Delhi – 110 017, India
Penguin Books (NZ), cnr Airborne and Rosedale Roads,
Albany, Auckland 1310, New Zealand
Penguin Books (South Africa) (Pty) Ltd, 24 Sturdee Avenue, Rosebank,
Johannesburg 2196, South Africa

Penguin Books Ltd, Registered Offices: 80 Strand, London WC2R 0RL, England

First published by Plume, a member of Penguin Group (USA) Inc.

First Printing, December 2004
10 9 8 7 6 5 4 3 2 1

Ⓟ REGISTERED TRADEMARK—MARCA REGISTRADA

LIBRARY OF CONGRESS CATALOGING-IN-PUBLICATION DATA

Hassler, Jon.
  [Staggerford murders]
  The Staggerford murders ; The life and death of Nancy Clancy's nephew / Jon Hassler.
    p. cm.
  ISBN 0-452-28540-2 (trade pbk.)
  1. Staggerford (Minn. : Imaginary place)—Fiction. 2. City and town life—Fiction.
3. Minnesota—Fiction. I. Hassler, Jon. Life and death of Nancy Clancy's nephew. II. Title.

PS33558.A726S74 2004
813'.54—dc22   2004050553

Printed in the United States of America
Set in Century Expanded

AUTHOR'S NOTE
A chapter from each of these novels appeared originally, in substantially different form,
in *The North American Review* and in my story anthology *Rufus at the Door*, published
by the Afton Historical Society Press.—JH

PUBLISHER'S NOTE
This is a work of fiction. Names, characters, places, and incidents either are the product of
the author's imagination or are used fictitiously, and any resemblance to actual persons, living or dead, business establishments, events, or locales is entirely coincidental.

For Dave and Joyce,
Carrie and Katie

THE
Staggerford
Murders

❖

Grover

※

I CAN TELL IT'S ONE OF THOSE MORNINGS when Dusty's at
loose ends and he's going to spend the day attached to me
like a bloodsucker. Thank the Lord this only happens about
once a week these days. Why, when Dusty first moved in, I'd
find him down here in the lobby every day waiting for me
when I came on duty. Not that he gets in the way or causes
trouble—no, he'll sit here in his baseball cap and overalls and
not say a word for hours on end, unless you get him started
on Caledonia—but how would you like to have somebody
watching every move you make from morning till night?

Today, for instance. Today's when the *Weekly* comes out.
I haven't missed reading every last word in the *Staggerford
Weekly* since 1945 when I came home from the war. I start
with the obituaries on the back page and make my way
frontwards through the weddings and letters to the editor
and the reports from the six or eight outlying villages, and
when I finish the front page I go back for a close reading of
the want ads. I can kill three hours easy on the *Weekly*. Well,
why not? As I've told Dusty more times than I care to re-

member, if you want to know what's going on in the outside world you've got to read the paper, but Dusty's got no time for the printed word. Caledonia used to take care of the reading for both of them, and since Caledonia died he depends on me to tell him what's what. Which I don't mind doing, but I hate to have him sitting here watching me turn the pages and criticizing my style. Last Thursday, for instance, just as I'm getting into the news from Loomis where it says that old Reverend Bunsen's widow's got this pileated woodpecker pecking away at a dead tree in her yard, Dusty up and tells me, "Cal'donie never used to move her lips when she read the paper." "Stick it in your ear," says I, under my breath.

Ollie Luuya up in two-ought-two—he's Dusty's nephew—claims I'm wasting my time, that the outside world is a lot bigger than Staggerford and I ought to be reading something else besides the *Weekly*, but Ollie's idea of reading material is Bible tracts and tales of near-death experiences and all that kind of folderol. I never knew Ollie in his days as a derelict, but I have a notion he probably wasn't quite so tiresome as he is since he got himself ordained.

Of course I have to admit there comes a Thursday now and again when you have to wonder if Ollie isn't right. Like today. There isn't a whole hell of a lot happened around here since last week's issue, and even the want ads are mostly ones I've seen before—Axel Johnson selling off his steers and heifers again so he and the wife can spend the winter in Phoenix; Miss Alicia Hitchkiss putting out the call for singers for her annual Christmas oratorio—but then all of a sudden I come upon this real interesting piece—a letter, not

4

to the editor, but to the people of Staggerford. It's on page two.

To whom it may concern,

I am writing this appeal to any and all citizens of Staggerford who remember my mother, Blanche Nichols, and who might be able to help me find her.

You will recall that she was last seen nine years ago this fall, working in her flower garden at Seven Hillcrest West. No clues ever turned up to indicate what became of her, so I am asking anyone with information concerning her disappearance or her whereabouts to write to me in care of this newspaper. Your letters will be forwarded to me and I will hold them in strictest confidence.

Sincerely,

Penny Jean Nichols
Fresno, California

"Hey, Dusty, here's a letter from that Nichols girl, her mother disappeared."

"Mmmm," says Dusty. He's dozing off. He's been falling asleep real easy lately—Doc Hammond lays it to his new heart medicine—especially when he settles into his easy chair. It's about the only piece of furniture he brought from home when he moved in here to the Ransford Hotel, and the reason it's down here in the lobby is it's too wide to get into his room. It's real ugly, upholstered in some sort of vegetation green and the sides leak stuffing where Caledonia's cats used to sharpen their claws, but Dusty loves sitting in it. Says it makes him think of Caledonia. He and Caledonia picked it up in the alley behind the Railroad Hotel back when the Railroad Hotel was a first-class place to stay and they were remodeling all their rooms. It wasn't long after that that passenger trains stopped coming through Staggerford and the Railroad Hotel went belly-up—a real satisfying development because most of their business came over here to the Ransford. Of course I'm talking ten years ago or more, before you had your motels out along the highway. Now the Ransford itself is going belly-up, they say.

When Mrs. Heffington stopped by the other day—she owns the place—she never said a thing about it, but she spilled the beans by saying that her lawyer asked her to ask me if I had a decent retirement plan. I haven't got a penny in retirement, not even social security, because her dead husband was always such a tightwad, but Mrs. Heffington isn't somebody you like to upset. She's one of those delicate old widows who seem to need protection from the facts of life, if you know what I mean. When you get into October like this, it gets pretty chilly in this lobby, and once I asked her if I could turn up the heat and she got all teary-eyed about how much money it would cost. Her husband, Ransford Heffington, was a regular old robber baron who owned half of downtown Staggerford before he died, but that still wasn't enough for him. About once a year he'd petition the city council to change the name of Staggerford to Heffington. Oh, he was a bearcat all right. Why, when I took over here as desk clerk—after they tore down the Morgan Hotel, where I used to work—Ransford Heffington told me that if I ever applied for social security he'd fire me on the spot. That's because your employer has to put in his share, and he was darned if he'd waste money on something like that.

I raise my voice. "Hey, Dusty, wake up! Remember a fellow named Nichols? He was the one got shot in front of the show house!"

Dusty comes to and says, "Yeh," but he just says it to be agreeable, I can tell.

"You don't have any idea who I'm talking about, do you?"

"Name rings a bell," he says.

"During Christmas week, in broad daylight, just as the matinee was letting out."

"Yeh," says Dusty.

"But it can't be nine years ago already. Five maybe. Six at the most."

"Five, six, somethin' like that," says Dusty.

"Come to think of it, Nichols used to be Ollie's boss at the Information Center." I shout upstairs, "Hey, Ollie!" at the top of my voice, which isn't loud enough to get him stirring.

I remind Dusty that Nichols was head man at the Chamber of Commerce in the days when Ollie used to be Staggerford's Indian. "People used to call him Eddie or Neddy or Teddy or something like that."

"Somethin' like that," says Dusty, rubbing his eyes. Then he gives me this alert, bloodshot look, as if he's thinking about staying awake until his afternoon nap. I've known Dusty Luuya for forty years. He's a Finlander and a retired garbageman. He's about three bricks short of a full load, if you catch my meaning, but he never seemed to mind being dumber than everybody else. He always worked hard, and he always had the most up-to-date truck in the entire garbage fleet. He made a decent living for himself and Caledonia. I heard he was having a hard time of it after Caledonia died, so I went over to his house and asked him why he didn't move into the Ransford, and that's all it took. He went into the bedroom for an extra pair of overalls and he came downtown with me. The next day we borrowed a pickup and went back and picked up his easy chair and a great big rock—he calls it a keepsake— and a few other items, and he's been living up in 213 ever since.

My new cordless phone rings and practically scares me out of my wits—I'm not used to carrying a telephone in my shirt pocket. Never mind if Ransford Heffington's been dead twelve, fourteen years, I still answer the phone the way he taught me. "Ransford Hotel, good morning, Grover speaking. Get a ten percent discount if you bring your own sheets." I myself added the part about the discount because if there's anything I hate worse than making beds it's going across the street to the Laundromat. This call's for Ollie, so I go to the stairway and holler his name.

"Yo," he answers, "I'll be right down."

The voice on the phone sounds like the Baptist reverend to me. I hope it's him wanting Ollie to preach on Sunday, because we're already ten days into the month and Ollie still hasn't paid his room rent. The Baptists'll give him twenty-five bucks for taking over a morning service, thirty-five for hanging around the whole day and handling the evening hoo-ha as well.

Ollie comes downstairs like he does every morning, so full of pep it makes you a little sick. "Good morning, Grover. Good morning, Uncle Dusty. Good morning, Lord, what a glorious morning to be alive. *This is the day the Lord has made,* and so forth. Hey, Grover, where's the telephone?"

I hand him my new cordless, and he looks pretty darn impressed.

"Wow, how long we had this?" he asks me.

"Since yesterday," I tell him.

"Then how come you're always crying for rent money if the hotel can afford a new cordless?"

This is the opening I've been waiting for all week. "Got it for my birthday," I tell him, but he doesn't pay any attention. He's saying hello and starts in conversing on the line. It's hell when the two friends you've got in the world don't remember your birthday. So I go back to my chair and tell Dusty. "Got the telephone from my cousin Henry's nephew, Henry Junior."

"Yeh," says Dusty.

"Turned eighty-one day before yesterday."

"I be danged."

"Unbelievable, huh?"

"Henry Junior don't look a day over sixty."

"Not Henry Junior! Me! I turned eighty-one."

"I be danged."

"You're no spring chicken yourself, Dusty. How old are you?"

He shrugs. "Sixty somethin', seventy, I don't know."

"You don't know? What year were you born?"

"It's on my driver's license."

"Let's see it."

"Lost it."

"You lost your driver's license? Hell's bells, Dusty, you've got to keep track of stuff better."

He blows his stack at this point. "I lost it, goddam it," he rages. "Now let me alone!" Dusty doesn't mind being criticized if it's anybody but me. Every time I try to set him straight he blows his cork.

"Hey, Uncle Dusty," says Ollie, who's hung up the phone by this time, "let's not be using the name of the Lord in vain."

I tattle on him. "He lost his driver's license."

"*Straighten up and fly right, sayeth the Lord, and beat thy anger into plowshares*—chapter one, Paul's letter to the Carpathians. That was Reverend Simley on the line."

"It sounded like that Baptist fellow."

"Nope, I'll never see the inside of that Baptist church again. We don't see eye-to-eye about the afterlife."

"You preaching heresy again?" I ask him. Ollie's got quite a streak of independence in him for a preacher.

"I just told his flock I didn't believe hell was really fire."

"What is it then?"

"Absence of God, plain and simple. And without God around to liven things up, eternity's going to get pretty darn boring." Ollie settles into the third easy chair in our little circle.

"So who's this new guy?" I ask him. "I never heard of a preacher named Simley."

"Deliverance Tabernacle, you know, out at the strip mall?"

"Never heard of it."

"It's out there where Monkey Wards catalogue store used to be. It's a fun church. They call themselves the Flock That Rocks. Say, Grover, did you put somebody up in two-oh-eight last night?"

"Yep, a couple young folks from out West."

"I thought I heard voices up there."

"Here, look at this." I hand him the newspaper, folded small so he sees the letter. He reads it while I wait for his reaction and his uncle Dusty sneaks in a little nap.

Finally Ollie says, "Hey, you know who this is? This is that Nichols girl that I used to work for her dad."

"That's what I was telling Dusty. He was shot out in front of the show house."

"I know. Susie Nesbitt was there."

"She was?" Susie Nesbitt's been Ollie's girlfriend off and on over the years. Mostly off.

"Sure. It was the kids' Christmas show, remember? Susie went to it. Neddy Nichols was shot in the chest, a twenty-two-caliber bullet right through the heart."

"Twenty-two caliber?" says I. "That ain't a very big bullet for killing a man."

Dusty speaks up: "I got me a rat gun that's a twenty-two revolver. Me and Cal'donie used to go out to the dump on summer nights and shoot rats."

"That's why the cops called it accidental homicide," says Ollie. "They figured anybody out to murder a man would be packing more power than a twenty-two. They said the shot might have come from one of the apartments over the stores in that block. Said some kid was probably playing with his twenty-two rifle and fired it off without meaning to."

Which is all a bunch of hogwash, far as I'm concerned. Ollie doesn't like to hear it, but I say it anyway. "From what I know about Edward W. Nichols, I'd say somebody wanted him rubbed out and got away with it."

"Oh, come on, Grover, think about it. They even had the state investigators in. This is hunting country. Most boys get their first twenty-two rifle when they're thirteen. They go out in the woods north of town and shoot squirrels and tin cans and songbirds."

"They go to the dump and shoot rats," Dusty adds.

But I don't back down. "It was a gangland murder. Nichols was into porn."

"Porn!" says Ollie, looking like he's been slapped in the face. "Who told you that?"

"It's well known that they found all those pictures in his office."

"Oh, for pity's sakes, Grover, you're way off base. Sure Mr. Nichols was a little weird, but who isn't? I mean, he used to bring pictures of naked people to work and stash them in his filing cabinet, but that doesn't mean he was mixed up with the Mafia."

"Then tell me this," says I. "The Nicholses built that humongous house over on the wealthy side of the Badbattle. Why, they had stuff you never saw in this town before. They had a two-story deck and a three-car garage and a gazz-a-bow out back big enough to hold a dance in."

"A what out back?"

"A gazz-a-bow, one of them outdoor rooms with screens on it?"

"A gazebo."

"Never mind, just tell me this. Where does the executive secretary of the Staggerford Chamber of Commerce get the money for a spread like that?"

"Well, for one thing, that was a good-paying job—thirty, forty thousand a year."

I give up. It's no use arguing with Ollie. I don't bother telling him that forty thousand bucks wouldn't have kept Mrs. Nichols in garden seeds. Why, her front yard was one big mass of flowers, clear down to the street. I heard tell her backyard was all gladiolies.

Ollie goes on, telling how it was Mrs. Nichols that built the house. He says her parents left her quite a little wad of money when they died. When he finishes, I have only one thing to say:

"Seems a shame—a woman like that, married to a porn king."

This really sets him off. "Listen, Grover, let's have a little respect. We're talking here about a man, a mortal man, who went to meet his maker before his time. 'And the dead you will always have with you, sayeth the Lord.' Paul's letter to the Theologians, chapter eighteen."

Dusty pipes up then. "Old man Nichols, his wife's dead, too, you know."

I ignore him when he talks nonsense, but Ollie always treats him like he's all there. He says, real gentlelike, "No, Uncle Dusty, we don't really know what happened to Mrs. Nichols."

"The flower lady over on Hillcrest? Oh, she's dead all right. Deader'n a doornail. I kilt her."

We all laugh at this crazy idea, even Dusty. Ollie says, "I agree it looks like foul play, Uncle Dusty. It wasn't six months after her husband was shot she just up and vanished off the face of the earth. What was it, Grover, June, July? Some neighbors out for their evening walk noticed there was nobody home at the Nichols house and the windows and doors were standing open and the sprinklers were going."

"Yes, it was summertime all right," says I, "but they got the year wrong in the paper. It was the year I had my varicose veins seen to, and that wasn't no nine years ago."

"It kind of gives you the willies, when you think about it," says Ollie. "The windows wide open, the flowers being watered. Chief of Police Morehouse said there was even the makings of supper laid out on the kitchen table."

"And Jell-O in the fridge," I tell him.

Ollie gives me this skeptical look, so I repeat it. "Jell-O in the fridge, fresh made."

"Who told you that?"

"Chief Morehouse. It had sliced bananas in it. Anyhow that don't matter. What matters is all those dirty pictures they found after Nichols died."

Now Ollie looks like he's on the verge of blowing his cork. "Listen, I'm sick and tired of people running Mr. Nichols into the ground. It was Neddy Nichols who made me what I am today."

I decide to push him over the edge, just for the fun of it.

"And what are you today, Ollie? You're a preacher without a church living in a hotel short of sheets."

His ears turn red, but he holds himself in by quoting the Bible. "Avoid storm and strife," he says. "Treat thy neighbor as thou wouldst be treated thyself. Geronimo, chapter three."

Ollie

❖

GROVER'S RIGHT, OF COURSE. It's just that I hate to think of myself as a derelict, which is what I used to be. I'm talking ten years ago, right after I came back from the war, and moved into a flophouse in Minneapolis. Well, I didn't see any other way. I was discharged from the army with a pretty serious case of the heebie-jeebies. It seemed like my motor was racing all the time, and yet I couldn't get enough sleep. I needed to go to bed every couple of hours, otherwise I'd start trembling and shaking. I still get the shakes a little bit if I get overtired, but that's gradually going away, thank the good Lord.

The flophouse was called the Soul's Arbor Hotel. Never mind the musty smell and the mice, it was the perfect place for me at that time of my life. It had a bed, a hot meal every day—or lukewarm anyway—and a live-in preacher by the name of Texas Jack Ashford. It was Texas Jack Ashford that first suggested I should go into the preaching game, said I ought to take some seminary training. I could see what a pipe dream that was—at least back then, in my disabled days. But the Lord works in mysterious ways. I told Texas Jack straight out, I said, No sir, preaching was clear out of my depth, and that's when Texas Jack asked me a question that changed my life. It's a question everybody ought to ask themselves whenever they're confused, stumped, or bamboozled. Five little words that can make all the difference.

He asked me, "Did you pray about it?"

Well, Lord help me, I hadn't even thought to pray about it. I don't suppose I'd prayed about anything since I was an eighth grader down the street here at St. Isidore's. So I did. I went up to my room and said, "Lord, I'm thinking about being a minister of your Gospel." And the Lord said, sort of sarcasticlike, "Yeah, right." By which I guess he meant I wasn't ready. At least that's the way I took it—it wasn't my time yet. But the seed was planted. A year or two years later, after I moved back here to Staggerford and got the job as tourist-center Indian, I started taking my seminary training. That was eight, nine years ago—I don't remember exactly. Grover would know. The nice thing these days is, you don't have to go away to college to become a freelance minister. You can do it by mail. I got my ordination papers from the Tallahassee Seminary of God in the Spirit. I asked Grover just the other day how long it's been since I moved in here at the Ransford.

"Ten years ago last spring," he said. "It was the year I had my ingrown toenail seen to. You went to work at the tourist center, and that's where you shoulda stayed. You never once came up short the first of the month till you took up the preaching racket."

I've taught myself to ignore Grover when he makes remarks like this. But today he's doesn't let up. He turns to Dusty and says, "Ollie'd be a decent sky pilot if he could reign himself in. He can't keep himself from rambling on and on."

This I can't ignore. "How do you know how I preach, Grover—you've never once come to hear me."

"Susie Nesbitt told me."

"Susie Nesbitt! Susie Nesbitt hasn't been inside a church for at least two years. I kicked her out, is what I did. She got to be so bossy and overbearing that every time I saw her in the congregation, I'd get tongue-tied. So I kicked her out, God forgive me." Susie Nesbitt's the main cog over at the Chamber of Commerce office. There's whole weeks go by when I don't dare walk past that place for fear Susie Nesbitt will see me out the window and come running after me to say my hair needs combing or my jacket's buttoned wrong.

She's been like that—overbearing—since she was a girl. She was always the bossiest kid in our class, intimidating our teachers until they gave up and did whatever she wanted them to do.

Ah, but I remember one time she met her match. It was back in junior high, when Sister Angeline was our teacher. Talk about a bossy, overbearing woman. Sister Angeline had a will like an iron bar. You have to realize how strict and religious school was back then, at least at St. Isidore's Junior High. Why heck, back then a St. Isidore's eighth grader was about the holiest person in your neighborhood. Each year, on the first of May everybody in the eighth grade wore white to school—white shirts and pants, white dresses, white socks, even white shoes if you had them, which I never did—and we marched in a procession from the classroom over to the church and up the middle aisle and over to the side altar, and Mary Catherine Corcoran, who was Queen of the May that year, stuck a bunch of flowers in a vase in front of the Blessed Virgin's statue.

May Day was the highlight of the year for Sister Angeline. You can read about May Day in books, and how it got started as a fertility ritual. It makes you think, doesn't it, how the church took it over and went the other direction with it. I mean, virginity instead of fertility. Honoring the statue of Mary instead of dancing around some phallic-looking maypole.

So anyhow, Susie Nesbitt decided she herself ought to be Queen of the May instead of Mary Catherine Corcoran, and she had a temper tantrum right there in class before we marched over to church. She wouldn't listen to reason. Sister Angeline's reason was that the honor belonged to someone named Mary each year, because being the Blessed Virgin's namesake made a girl especially pleasing in the sight of God. Susie Nesbitt wasn't used to being denied. You could tell that by the way she started screaming, but there was no budging Sister Angeline. I wondered at the time, and I still wonder, why Susie put up more of a fuss than the other three Marys in class who'd been passed over. I guess it was Mary Catherine Corcoran's peerless grade-point average that made her queen. I wondered, too, if it would have made a difference had Sister Angeline known that Mary Catherine had been letting boys diddle her in the grove of trees behind the blacksmith's shop since the sixth grade.

In those days we were brought up with a heavy dose of

church, and it sticks to you like Velcro. I guess quite a few of my classmates stayed Catholic, while I found another way. But aren't we all brothers and sisters under the skin? *Amen, I say to you, Lutherans and Hottentots shall lie down together like lambs in the peaceable kingdom.* Paul's letter to the Romanians, chapter twelve.

When I first moved back to Staggerford, we both worked in the tourist center out on Highway 71, Susie and I. My job was to sit in a chair all day, outside under the overhang, and look like a dignified Ojibway. I'd have my picture taken with brides and fishermen and drunks and I'd listen to the same dumb questions day after day. "Are you a hunter-gatherer?" "Do your people still hate the Sioux?" "Do you live in a wigwam?" Susie worked inside. She was the clerk in the gift shop and she directed tourists to the many lake resorts in the area.

Because the tourist center was run by the Chamber of Commerce, our boss was Mr. Edward W. Nichols. His nickname was Neddy, but I never called him that. I called him Mr. Nichols. I always liked him. He was a quiet sort of guy who minded his own business and let you tend to yours. We never saw much of him out there beside the highway. Once in a while he'd stop by on his way out of town and roll down his window and ask how things were going. He usually had his daughter, Penny Jean, with him, sometimes his wife. I always told him things were going swell, even if Susie was squabbling with a customer in the gift shop, which happened about every other day, it seemed to me.

Susie's Nesbitt's trouble was perfectionism. It still is. Say a stranger showed up looking like something the cat dragged in—say he'd driven all the way from Chicago nonstop—she'd tell him to tuck in his shirt and wipe the scowl off his face. One time old Mrs. Heffington came in—Mrs. Heffington owned the property the tourist center sits on, and to this day she owns this Ransford Hotel, which was named after her husband, Ransford B. Heffington. Susie pointed out how Mrs. Heffington had applied her rouge higher on one cheek than the other. It was this abrasiveness that, in the end, got Susie promoted. After several complaints to the Chamber, especially Mrs. Heffington's complaint, Mr. Nichols moved Susie into his office on Main Street and made her his receptionist and secretary. Then didn't she preen! She still does. With her beaky nose and small, close-set eyes, she walks along the street like a preening bird.

Of course I have to admit it was Susie Nesbitt who brought me home. I mean, I was living the life of a derelict more or less, and it was Susie called me on the telephone and said the Chamber of Commerce was looking for a new Indian. "You got the wrong number," I told her. "There aren't any Indians here at Soul's Arbor."

But she insisted. She said, "You're the one we're after, Ollie. Sit outside the tourist center the way French Lopat used to. We've had an Indian sitting there since nineteen forty-six."

"You got the wrong guy," I told her. "I'm not Indian."

"Your hair is still black, isn't it? Listen, Ollie, it's the easiest job in the world. Just put on the feathers and the deerskin vest and sit there and stare at people."

I hung up on her. It was kind of nice hearing her voice though. It took me back and made me think of all the people I used to like in Staggerford. About two minutes later, she called me back to tell me more about the job benefits. She said the Chamber would pay me five bucks an hour and they were cutting it down from six to five days a week. All I had to do was show up by ten in the morning, and I could knock off any time after four. Plus, another benefit was that I'd get fired every September so I could draw unemployment over the winter.

I was mightily tempted by the thought of earning around thirty dollars a day just sitting in a chair, but I had to remind her I wasn't an Indian, I was a Finlander. She said, "So what, neither was French Lopat. All you've got to do is *look* like an Indian."

"What's wrong with French?" I asked her. "He looks more like an Indian than I do." French Lopat, who'd had the job for ten years or more, was said to be the love child of somebody from St. Paul.

"French quit," she said. "He got a job delivering mail."

"Okay, Susie," says I. "If you send me bus fare, I'll try it for a few days." Those few days turned into a year and a half, and then I sent away for my ordination papers, and I'm still here. The Lord works in mighty mysterious ways, Paul's letter to the Filipinos, chapter one, verse two.

Dusty

❖

ALL THE WHILE Grover and Ollie are sittin' here shootin' the bull, I'm havin' myself a little heart attack. I've probably had a dozen heart attacks in my life, and on account of Cal'donie puttin' up such a fuss every time, I got so I like to keep 'em to myself. But the minute I take out my medicine bottle and try shakin' a nitro into my hand, Grover figures out what's goin' on and he starts fussin' just the way Cal'donie used to, and of course that gets Ollie all excited and they start jabberin' over me like bluejays. If you ask me, they're both a couple of downright fussbudgets.

"Here, Dusty, take these!" says Grover, grabbin' the pill bottle out of my hand and droppin' three nitros in my mouth.

"He needs medical attention," says Ollie.

"No, it's only his angie peccadoris acting up," says Grover. "These nitro pills take care of it just fine."

I put out my hand for more pills—I usually take five or six of the little buggers—but he says, "No, Doc says three's the limit." So I grab his shirt and pull so hard a button comes flyin' off, and he says, "It's a bad one, eh, Dusty?" and I nod my head and he gives me one more.

Meanwhile Ollie keeps sayin' I need medical attention and Grover keeps sayin', "No, he's feeling better already, aren't you, Dusty?" And as a matter of fact, I am. But Ollie grabs Grover's telephone and starts dialin' for help. So you can see why I like to keep my heart attacks to myself.

It's a couple of minutes before the pain goes completely away and Grover and Ollie settle down to talkin' about Mr. Nichols again. This is a real interestin' subject to me, because Cal'donie spent so much time researchin' the Nichols family. I speak up and tell the two of em, "You know what? Cal'donie figured out who kilt that Nichols fella."

This shuts 'em up for a minute, but they don't look like they believe me. They look like they think I'm nuts. So I go on. I tell them what else I know. "We used to know who kilt Mrs. Nichols, too. It was me. Only her name wasn't Nichols anymore by that time."

Grover says, "You're wrong, Dusty. Nobody knows what happened to Mrs. Nichols. Nobody ever said she's dead. She just left town on the spur of the moment."

"Oh, she's dead all right," I tell him. "I kilt her, but I forget just how it happened. It'll come to me—just give me a minute. Only by the time she died she was hooked up with some other fellow, name of Gower or Bauer or some such name."

My nephew Ollie speaks up then and says, "Hey, Grover, he's right. She married a guy named Bauer, remember? George Bauer. He's still living in the Nichols house."

The way it all started, I was the Nichols' garbologist. I

had Hillcrest West on my route, but I didn't think a thing of it until I married Cal'donie Wolsey and she pointed out that I was pickin' up the best grade of garbage in town. Shucks, before I met Cal'donie, garbage was garbage to me.

I go ahead and tell Ollie and Grover the story, startin' at the beginnin'. I tell them about how, on Thursdays, when I made my run through the alleys of Hillcrest, Cal'donie'd be sittin' up there beside me in the truck, admirin' all them fancy backyards. I don't think she ever once climbed down out of the cab. She was well satisfied to let me inspect the garbage. I knew her taste ran to jewelry mainly, and readin' matter. By jewelry I don't mean diamonds and rubies and such. You won't find precious stones in people's garbage. I'm talkin' about bigger, cheaper pieces, the kind a woman can wear on her coat.

Two of her favorites I come across on the same day. One was a big-eyed owl sittin' on a silver moon crescent. One of the owl's eyes was missin', but we had scads of rhinestones in a recipe box at home, and we found one about the right size and glued it in the socket and Cal'donie wore it to wrestlin' that night and four of her friends said how nice it looked. The other one was a piece of squiggly brass that Cal'donie said looked like a capital *W,* but at bingo that weekend somebody said it looked more like a capital *E.* So after that she wore it upside down and it looked great. It didn't look like nothin'.

Cal'donie, she was a wise old dame—for a waitress. I mean that's all she ever was, was a waitress, until I come along and took her up into the leisure class. That's when she really blossomed out.

Why, when she become a full-time garbologist's wife, she took to culture like a cockroach to syrup. You never seen nobody that loved the printed word the way Cal'donie did. From the day she moved in with me till the day before she died she kept an up-to-date file of the Minneapolis *Star-Tribune*. She had the *Staggerford Weekly* going back to 1968. She kept the St. Paul *Pioneer Press* too, but that was more hit and miss, 'cuz there was only one or two people on my route that took that paper, and if there was somethin' sticky or smelly wrapped up in it, I'd let it alone.

After she died, I started hauling the papers to the dump. I never said this to Cal'donie, but I was never too crazy about having all that stuff in the house, especially after we had to close off the front parlor, it was that full of paper. I wasn't crazy about all them letters neither, even if they didn't take up so much room. She had 'em pretty well sorted out as to whose garbage they come out of, and she kept 'em in the china cabinet. She liked to go over old mail in the evenin' and try to stump me by readin' a letter and askin' me whose garbage it come out of. I got so I was right about half the time.

I hauled all the letters to the dump, too, as long as I was at it. Well, cripes, you never know who might come snoopin' through your house someday and take up them letters and put two and four together the way Cal'donie did the time she solved the Nichols murder mystery.

The Nicholses' was one of them places where the garbage was always worth a close look. Our best tablecloth come from there, along with no end of fancy whiskey bottles, and the twenty-two revolver we used to shoot rats with at the dump. Cal'donie kept a complete file of Nichols mail—it was that interestin'. I mean after the first one, from that doctor out West, how could you pass anything up?

I'll never forget the day I found it. Mrs. Nichols already had her new husband by that time. He was a big guy who always wore a cowboy hat. We'd seen him sniffin' round the place even before old man Nichols was shot. It was the first really warm day in spring and I snatched up the letter and wiped the grease off it—you'd be surprised how many people throw their mail out with their table leavings—and I handed it up to Cal'donie in the cab. She read it while I worked my compactor.

Not all your garbologists have got the honest-to-goodness compactor in the rear end of their truck. They might say they got one, but all they really got back there is a pusher. A pusher works like a paddle wheel, pushing the garbage forward to the front of the truck so it don't all pile up at the back end, but a compactor actually squeezes the trash together so you don't have to make but half the trips to the dump that everybody else does. I had one of the first real compactors in the business in them days. It wasn't one of them heavy-duty jobs you see in junkyards that can press a car down to the size of a bicycle, but it was a real work-saver, and it was fun to monkey with. When I had time to work it just right, I could get a good-sized dog to fit in a shoebox.

So anyhow, I tightened up my load and climbed up behind the wheel and Cal'donie says the letter comes from a place in Sacramento, California, called the Dell Rapids Clinic, and while I coast downhill to my next stop she reads it to me.

"Dear Mrs. Nichols," it says. "Penny Jean's condition remains stable."

"Who's Penny Jean?" I ask.

"Penny Jean is Mrs. Bauer's daughter by her first husband, now hush up, don't interrupt," says Cal'donie, and she goes on readin'. "Well over three months have passed since her last episode, and she remembers absolutely nothing about the events of December twenty-third. Medication, as I insisted from the beginning, is much more effective than psychotherapy in cases like hers, and I thank you for your faith in our clinic."

That much I remember by heart. The rest of it went on to say that if Penny Jean didn't have any more episodes, she'd be released into Mrs. Bauer's custody around the first of October. Then it went on to say a curious thing. It said like this: "I hope by this time you have explained this troublesome situation to Mr. Bauer, and that when Penny Jean is released you will both come for her." It said, "Yours truly," and was signed by some doctor or other of the Dell Rapids Clinic.

Grover and Ollie sit up and take notice when I tell 'em all this, so I go ahead and tell 'em the rest of it. I tell 'em how a year or two later we're settin' there in front of the TV havin' supper and Cal'donie puts down her spoon and gives me her wise look and she asks me a question. She says, out of the clear blue, "Why do you suppose George is bein' kept in the dark?" "George who?" says I. "George Bauer, Mrs. Nichols' new husband," she says, and she quotes from the letter: " 'I assume by this time you have explained this troublesome situation to Mr. Bauer.' " And then she says, "Wouldn't you think George Bauer would know about his own stepdaughter bein' in a nuthouse?" "Well, you'd sure think so," says I, "we know it and we ain't even related." "Well, figure it out," says Cal'donie. "The reason is, she hasn't wanted to tell him her daughter is a nutcase. You do the dishes. I got some research to do."

So while I threw out the sardine tins and washed up the little plastic containers ready-made Jell-O comes in, Cal'donie went to work in the parlor. She worked till bedtime and again the next morning, and by the time I come home for lunch she had it down pat. "You know why Mrs. Nichols isn't telling George about her daughter being a nutcase?" she says. "Because it was her daughter killed her husband." Well, you could have knocked me over with a lead pipe.

"Why else would the poor girl be farmed out with the loonies practically the next day after her daddy's shot? Listen here," she says, and she reads from a newspaper. " *'Penny Jean, Penny Jean,' a high-pitched voice screamed in the sudden silence following the crack of a shot. It was the voice of Mrs. Nichols, the victim's wife, and to this day nothing more is known about last winter's daring daylight murder of Edward W. Nichols, executive director of the Staggerford Chamber of Commerce.*"

Then she shows me the pitcher in the paper. There's the missus all right, kneeling on the sidewalk, and behind her I see a young girl about fourteen years old about to step inside the show house. "That there's Penny Jean," says Cal'donie. "It says so under the pitcher. I 'spect she's going in to see if there's any candy left. See what it says there on the marquee— *3 STOOGES, FREE XMAS MOVIE, FREE XMAS CANDY.*"

"Did we see that show?" I ask.

"Never mind. Now you listen to this, Dusty. Mrs. Nichols told the cops that her husband dashed across the street to the show house to beat a traffic light, and she and her daughter hung back on the curb, and Mr. Nichols was just openin' the door to the show house when the show lets out and this great yappin' pack of kids come rushin' out gobblin' their X-mas candy, and I bet you any amount of money that's where Penny Jean shoots him, at close range. Bullet goes in right between the ribs and into his heart and he's dead before he hits the ground."

"But you just said Penny Jean hung back across the street."

"Don't be dumb, Dusty. Her mother just *claimed* she was across the street to keep her out of trouble. See, what I think is that the girl hurried across with her daddy and did the deed and the mother lied and the cops believed her."

"Then how come nobody saw her do it?"

Cal'donie's got an answer to that, too. "It's the eve of X-mas Eve, Dusty. That's the day this town goes nuts tryin' to get their hands on the last dollar X-mas shoppers have got left in their pocket. Free movies for the kids, free candy, free lutefisk at Druppers' Grocery. In a crowd like that, who notices what you do? Lordy, nobody even knew there was a dead man on the sidewalk until they felt him underfoot."

"Well then, why is Nichols goin' to a kids' movie in the first place? Most grown-ups don't even like The Three Stooges."

"He isn't going to the movie, Dusty, he's in charge of it.

The eve of X-mas Eve is sponsored by the Chamber of Commerce."

"And what about the gun? Somebody must've seen her standin' there with the gun in her hand."

"That's a mystery nobody figured out."

"You mean they never found the murder weapon?"

"How could they? We got it."

"Our rat gun?"

Cal'donie nods and says, "Our twenty-two revolver." She's quick all right, but there's one question I bet she don't have the answer to, and that's why: "Why'd she do it, Cal'donie? You gotta have a pretty strong reason to shoot your own daddy."

But by golly she's got an answer for that, too. "Nutcases don't *need* reasons," she says.

Some people, if they knowed what we knowed, would of gone to the cops. I ask Grover and Ollie if they know Buddy Long. 'Course they do, Buddy Long's caretaker of the Staggerford dump grounds. His main job is coverin' up what you dump. You back up to the pit and dump your load and next thing here comes Buddy zippin' along on his backhoe and he smooths it over and packs it down nice as you please. Cale'donie was always after me to try for Buddy's job. He gets first look at the whole town's garbage and takes home whatever he wants. I ain't sayin' Buddy's a troublemaker or anything, it's just that he's the kinda guy who'll call the cops the minute he sees something the least bit out of the way. Cal'donie always said if you mind your own business the cops will mind theirs and never the twain shall meet.

But I tell you who I felt sorry for. I felt sorry for Mrs.

Nichols. Blanche was her name. She had this brand-new husband, George Bauer—so what? He was never around. As many times as we stopped in their alley, we seen him only a coupla times, and I think those coupla times was before her first husband was did in. I don't know how she knew it, but Cal'donie claimed from the get-go that Mrs. Nichols and George Bauer were playin' hanky-panky.

'Course now you can see George Bauer and his new missus anytime you want to. He's retired and living in that same house with this new blondie of his. It wasn't even a month after Mrs. Nichols disappeared that he turned up with this new Mrs. Bauer. Grover tells me she's in the paper practically every week for rollin' high game down at Lilac Lanes.

Grover

❖

A T THIS POINT a guy walks in off the street. I'm about to
raise the stakes and tell him, "Fifteen percent off if you
bring your own sheets," when he hollers out, real grufflike,
"Who's in charge of this fleabag?"

"Hold your shirt on," I tell him, stepping over to the registration counter. He's a great, big, white-haired guy wearing a ten-gallon hat on his head and a sneer on his lips, like
he's gone through life feeling superior to everybody he's
ever met. He's got a goatee. He wants to know who stayed
at the hotel last night. At first I figure he's the father of one
of the young couple from out West, but it turns out he's looking for Penny Jean Nichols. I tell him he's only about two or
three thousand miles off base, that Penny Jean Nichols lives
clear out in California. I just read about her in the paper. "I
know where she lives," he says, real perturbedlike. "What I
want to know is where she's staying."

"Well, she ain't here."

"Are you sure?"

"Look, there's only four rooms occupied," I tell him, stepping around the counter and opening the registration book. "Ollie Luuya, Dusty Luuya, a fellow named Grover—that's me—and some people from out West name of Sanderson—not that it's any of your darn business."

At this he gets real nasty. I guess I asked for it, but I hate it when people get high-handed with me. He says, "Let me talk to somebody who knows what's going on around here!"

"You're talking to him. I'm in charge here . . ."

"Listen, I happen to know from the editor of the *Weekly* that Penny Jean Nichols is staying at your hotel."

"I don't care what the editor says. Here, look for yourself."

He gives me a sneer and turns and starts upstairs. I tell him to stop, he's got no business up there, but he says, "Try and stop me," and keeps on going.

He's about halfway up the steps when Dusty pipes up and says, "Now it comes back to me how I kilt Blanche." This stops the big guy in his tracks. He stands there listening. Ollie's sitting with his back to the stairs so he doesn't see him, and if Dusty notices he doesn't let on.

Dusty

❖

NOW IT COMES BACK TO ME how I kilt Blanche . . . I tell
Ollie and Grover about it. One Thursday after a hard
frost, me and Cal'donie saw Blanche pullin' up the stems of
dead flowers by her back door and I told Cal'donie she ought
to get out of the truck and strike up a friendship with her. I
said Blanche would be glad to have somebody she could talk
to about the murder, instead of keepin' it all to herself, but
Cal'donie said Blanche wasn't her type, and besides, she'd
lost interest in the case now that she had it solved.

"But Cal'donie," I said. "Just think what the poor dame is
going through. She's got a lot on her mind, keepin' that secret all the time. Maybe if she talked it over with you, she'd
have an easier time telling George."

"Far as I'm concerned, what's done is done," says
Cal'donie, and I'm sure that would of been her last word on
the subject—if I didn't bring Blanche home with me the next
week. It was the end of September, right before Penny Jean
was supposed to get out of the hospital. I went to Hillcrest
alone because Cal'donie had the flu and she wanted to stay

home close to the toilet. Blanche was out by her back door again, sweeping leaves off her patio. I stopped the truck in the alley same as usual and she never paid the least attention. A word to the wise saves nine, they always say, so I decided to tell her what I thought of keepin' George in the dark. Standin' next to her garbage cans I said, not very loud, "Blanche."

She looked up with her mouth kind of hangin' open, surprised. Have I said she wasn't a bad lookin' woman for her time in life? We stood there starin' at each other across the backyard for maybe two seconds. I knew what was goin' through her mind. She's wonderin' how in the world her garbologist knows her name. Then she goes back to sweepin'.

"Blanche," I call out, louder than before—louder than I need to because she gives a little cry and drops her broom. She comes toward me with her head cocked to one side, like a pup, and she seems to be smilin', but when she gets close I see she isn't. She's got the wrinkles in her forehead all twisted up—that look people get when they're surprised and scared at the same time. She says she doesn't believe we've met.

I ask her, "How's George?"

"George is fine," she says. "Do you know George?"

"I hardly ever see him around here."

"He's out in front putting in sod," she says, lookin' like she's told me a lie so I'll think her husband's around to protect her. Then she starts walkin' backward and then she turns and runs to her back door. I'm afraid she'll go inside before I get it off my chest, so I holler at her as she's pickin' up her broom. What I say is, "Tell George about what Penny Jean did or you'll be sorry."

They were words with a pretty strong effect. She turned wild. She come down off them steps at a run, shouting, "Who told you about Penny Jean? She's ready to come home!" "I know it," I say just as she stabs me in the chest with the broom handle and she breaks one or two of my ribs. She rears back to poke me again, but I get ahold of her wrists and I sit her down on the grass. Then I let her have it in the forehead with my fist.

Then she died.

I knew she was dead by the way she laid there, limp as a chloroformed cat. I don't know if I could of been arrested for that or not. She hit first.

All the while I'm tellin' this, Ollie has a real stern look on his face, and Grover sits there with his mouth hangin' open like he never heard it before. And I guess he never did, at that, because I never told it before. So I go on and tell them about how I figured out right away that I was in trouble, so I crawled up and sat in my truck with the door shut, trying to think what Cal'donie would of done in a case like this. Lucky for me, the backyard was surrounded by a bunch of high bushes and the only people that could of saw me was the neighbors to the east and they weren't home. They hadn't set out garbage for two weeks.

It bothered me that Blanche was lyin' there dead, though, and I'd about decided to load her in the truck and take her home and let Cal'donie figure out what to do with her when I had this vision. In my outside mirror I saw Mr. Bauer come in sight wheelin' a load of dirt and rocks in a wheelbarrow, and he stopped and stared when he saw Blanche lyin' there by the back of the truck. Then I saw Blanche come back to life. It was like a miracle, because after I kilt her she started raisin' her head up off the ground, and when Mr. Bauer saw her movin' he took a big rock from his wheelbarrow and dropped it on her head. That snuffed her for good. I looked at her layin' dead there for a minute and then I got out of the truck to talk it over with Mr. Bauer, to see if he minded if I took her away with me, but when I got out behind the truck he was nowhere to be seen. There was just Blanche and me. That's when I figured out he never *was* there, and what I saw was a vision. There was a nice big rock layin' nearby that I didn't notice before. It had a pretty streak of red on it darker than ketchup, more the color of Heinz 57. I knew Cal'donie'd like it, so I lifted it into the truck along with Blanche and took the afternoon off.

When I got home, Cal'donie said she liked the rock just fine, but I done the wrong thing. She said I should of left Blanche right where she was. I said I could take her back, but Cal'donie said that would be worse yet. The cops can tell if a body's been moved, and no end of trouble comes from movin' bodies. We were standin' at the tailgate looking in at Blanche lyin' there on top of everything she'd threw out. Her good looks were pretty well spoiled. Her forehead was all black where it was bashed in. Boy, I never knew I had that much power in my fist. Well, Cal'donie didn't look so hot herself, crawlin' out of her sickbed and standin' there in the driveway barefoot. She hemmed and hawed for a long time till I finally said, "Look here, tell me what to do and I'll do it. I don't want to worry about this overnight."

Cal'donie said, "Okay, scrunch her up so she fits in a leaf bag."

So that's what I done. It took only four squeezes of my compactor. The hard part was crawlin' in there between squeezes and turning her lengthwise. It was hard because my ribs hurt. Slipping her inside the first bag was tricky because she had a couple of splintered bones that kept tearing the plastic, but with Cal'donie's help we got her bundled up good. We tied one bag shut and then slipped her into another until she was inside five or six bags.

"What if the bags bust when I dump her?" I said.

"You can't dump her with only that little bit of garbage," she said. "Look at all that blood. If you dump a full load she won't be so noticeable."

I looked at my watch. "I can't get a load before the dump closes. It will take me that long to get over to Hillcrest and back."

"For this, anybody's garbage will do," she said. "Now get goin'."

So I tore through the neighborhood on the way to the dump, scatterin' cans ever which way. Most of the cans were only half full, so it took me twice as many stops to fill the truck. And every time I picked one up, the pain in my side took my breath away. It felt like Blanche was still jabbin' me with her broomstick.

I got to the dump before the gate closed all right, but I had to wait my turn to unload. There's always a lineup of trucks if you get there around closin' time. Some garbologists'll keep their load at home overnight and go to the dump first thing in the mornin' when it's not so crowded, but I've never been one to do that. I don't believe in carryin' around yesterday's garbage.

When it came my turn, I backed up to the edge of the pit and raised the box and dumped. Then I got out and looked down in the pit. Blanche was the biggest item in my load so she was easy to spot.

She looked to me like she had a sharp leg bone stickin' out through all them layers of black plastic, but otherwise the package held together just fine. Buddy Long come chuggin' over on his front-end loader. It's the new yellow machine Caterpillar makes, and you can tell by the way Buddy drives it that he enjoys his work. He covered my load with two scoops of dirt, then he drove over it a few times to tamp it down. He looked up and waved at me, and I waved back in spite of the catch in my side.

You know, it feels like my ribs never did heal right. Now all this time later, I still can't lift my right arm as high as my left. Cal'donie used to say it was a reminder not to get personal with my customers. That Cal'donie, she was a real card.

Grover

❖

THOSE ARE THE LAST WORDS out of Dusty's mouth, because the next minute he's having himself a granddaddy
of a heart attack. It spills him out of his chair and onto the
floor and I tell Ollie he'd better call 911 again and find out
what happened to that ambulance and Ollie says, no, there
isn't time, it looks like his uncle's checking out, so he's going
to take him to the hospital in his car.

Then a lot of stuff happens at once. There's a siren comes
blaring down the street, and my telephone starts ringing,
and the young woman up in 219 comes out onto the landing
and hollers down to ask what all the commotion is about, and
this big guy on the stairs, the minute he hears her voice, he
perks up and turns and looks up at her with this big, shit-
eating grin on his face, and the two of them get into a spat
and the siren stops outside in front of the hotel and two
medics come in and load Dusty on a stretcher and take him
out to the ambulance. Ollie leaves with his uncle.

I press the green button on my telephone to answer it,
but I don't say anything because the spat between the big

guy and the young woman is so interesting to listen to. I stoop down behind the registration counter so I can't be seen. He says, "What's the matter, Penny Jean, don't you recognize me?" and she just stands there staring down at him with a hateful look in her eye. He says, "Well, it's been what, almost ten years since you've seen me? I'm George Bauer, darlin'," and he puts out his hand to her and she hollers, "I know who you are, you creep. Don't touch me!"

He doesn't lose a bit of his cool. He says, "My one regret in life is that my time with your mother was much too short." And this sets her off hollering again. "Where is my mother?" she screams. "What did you do with my mother?"

"It's the greatest coincidence," he says, just as calm as you please. "I came downtown today to propose that you and I join forces to find out what happened to my dear Blanche, to your dear mother. And would you believe it? Not two minutes ago, right here, waiting for you to come downstairs, I learned what became of her."

Penny Jean says, "Tell me, where is she?" But George doesn't tell her. He says, "Oh, trust me, you don't want to know where she is. But you'll be glad to know she spent her last happy moments on this earth in the garden."

"She's dead?" Penny Jean looks like she's had the wind punched out of her. But she recovers fast. Next thing, she screams at him, "You killed her!" and she turns and hollers up the stairs, "Sandy!" It's amazing how George doesn't become the least bit riled up. He says, "Killed her? Is that any way to talk to your stepfather? Oh, you're a little heartbreaker, you are." And he takes a step up, toward her, which seems to scare her. She says, "Stay away from me, you creep," and she calls "SANDEEEE" again, and then she says, "How did you know I was here?"

This guy's a wonder. He just keeps on explaining things to her no matter how she bad-mouths him. "Your whereabouts are common knowledge at the newspaper office, Penny Jean. Coming from a city like Fresno, of course, you wouldn't understand the difficulty of keeping a secret in a town this size. That's why your mother was such a marvel. Keeping the truth not only from the local stumblebums, but from the state investigators as well."

There's quite a little silence then, before Penny Jean asks, "What do you mean?" If she hadn't said it, I'd of had to speak up and ask myself, I was that curious. He answers, "Absolutely incredible how convincing she was, how stalwart, so you could go about your life undisturbed. Oh, yes, she did, she covered for you to the bitter end, Penny Jean." Penny Jean says, "You're out of your mind. I didn't do anything," and he comes back with, "But you conspired, my dear. You were part of the plot. Not that you both weren't justified of course. I mean, to be sexually abused by your own flesh-and-blood father? Well, when your mother found out, she was a mighty upset little woman, let me tell you. But once the two of you killed him, she never looked back. The very next day she whisked you out to California to the Dell Rapids Clinic and Retreat Center, and she told everybody you were out there in prep school. It's one of the regrets of my life that you were gone during my time with your dear mother."

Penny Jean breaks down then. There are tears in her eyes and her voice is shaky, but she's still mad as a hornet.

She says, "Listen, you ass, I did not shoot my father, and the Dell Rapids Clinic is a fraud."

George says, "Ah, but you're forgetting your happy times there. Swimming, horseback riding, climbing, hiking. I still have the sweet, pathetic letter you wrote me from Dell Rapids."

Penny Jean says she never wrote him a letter in her life, but he insists. He says, "Of course you did. Your mother was late with a payment, remember? And you wrote, begging me to keep paying for your residence at Dell Rapids. You were quite distraught at the idea of having to leave. Well, I mean, who can a poor orphan count on if not her own stepfather?"

Penny Jean admits it then. "So what if I wrote you a letter? I was medicated to the eyeballs. My life was set back years at the Dell Rapids Clinic. Can you imagine anything stupider than trying to cure a person by erasing her memory?"

George says, "Ah, but you were happy enough to be there while I was paying for it."

Penny Jean shoots back, "With my mother's money! Or have you forgotten where your livelihood comes from—you and your new Barbie Doll, living in the house that belongs to me."

"Ah," he says, "so you know Margie then."

It's then that her smart mouth gets her in trouble. "Everybody who reads the Staggerford paper knows Margie Bauer, the bowling queen of Lilac Lanes. She turned up in the newspaper about a week after you got rid of my mother."

Now it's his turn to holler. He's mad. "You have a very

smart mouth, for a murderer on the loose!" He crowds her up the steps and she screams, "Sandy, come here! Quick!" Sandy's obviously the name of her husband or boyfriend, you never know these days, and sure enough, he turns up and starts swinging at George. He's kind of a short squirt, and George is a lot bigger and stronger. He grabs the kid by the wrists and he says, "Listen, you California pervert, you're playing with dynamite. I was all-conference fullback for the Minnesota Gophers."

You can tell Sandy isn't all that impressed because he keeps struggling to get his hands free. He gives George a kick in the leg that makes him tighten his grip on the kid. He says, "Listen now, Sandy-wandy, I'm going to tell you something about your sweetheart that you probably never knew. Your sweetheart Penny Jean conspired with her mother to shoot her father dead in the street. The way it worked, Penny Jean's mother was the actual murderer, she pulled the trigger, and immediately dropped the revolver into Penny Jean's purse and Penny Jean ran off and disposed of it. I know all about it because I was there. I saw it happen, right in front of the Paramount Theater. Nine years ago Christmastime."

Penny Jean says, "You did not! You weren't anywhere near the theater!"

"But of course I was, Penny Jean." He's gone back to his gentle voice. "I saw the whole thing from next door, standing in front of the hardware store. Well, I mean, how could I pass up the chance to see an actual murder? And don't forget, I had a vested interest in your little drama. One, it was my revolver, after all. And two, I was the stand-in for your father when you rehearsed it at home. Or did they teach you to forget that as well?"

"Oh, yes, I remember how you encouraged her all along the way," says Penny Jean. "You see, after a lot of painful counseling, I've recovered my memory. You're as guilty as my mother was, George Bauer."

But I don't think he hears this part because Sandy has started to struggle again, and this time he gets loose and takes a swing at George, and George ducks and drops him with one punch to the face. Penny Jean screams and runs to Sandy and helps him up to their room, him dripping blood out of his nose all over the steps. George Bauer turns and goes out the door, letting in a whole bunch of cold air, and he stands there on the sidewalk, lighting a cigar. The ambulance is gone by this time, so I'm alone at last. I say hello into the telephone. "Ransford Hotel, Grover speaking," I say. "Twenty percent discount if you bring your own sheets," but nobody's on the other end.

Uh-oh. George Bauer opens the door again and comes back inside. I duck down behind the counter because he's a hothead and a lot stronger than I am, and I'm damned if I'm going to get mixed up in his family problems.

George Bauer

❖

I'VE GOT MORE TO SAY to my stepdaughter, but rather than deal with her puny mouse of a companion, I wait in the lobby for her. The lobby's empty, the three guys gone. The young preacher must've gone off with the sick garbageman, and the old desk clerk has disappeared as well. If the garbageman dies, I'll know for sure that fate is playing into my hands. He's the only person who saw the rock lying beside Blanche's head and he's too stupid to realize it's what I finished her off with. I wish he hadn't told these two goons about it, but they're both probably as dim-witted as he is.

I sit on a couch so worn out you can feel the springs under your ass, and I read the only magazine in sight, an old copy of *Sports Illustrated*, from cover to cover. Still she doesn't come down. Well, I've got all day. I stretch out on the couch and doze off for twenty minutes and then I hear randy Sandy come down the stairs and call to Penny Jean. "Hey, Penny, you coming?" he shouts, and she says, "Give me two minutes," and he says, "Okay, I'll bring the car around front." He goes out the door, so he doesn't hear her calling down to him,

"We won't need the car. The police station is just down the block and the newspaper office is across the street." When she finally comes down, she doesn't notice me sitting here. She about shits her pants when I speak up. "Well, Penny Jean," I say, "you certainly take your sweet time coming downstairs, I've missed my lunch."

She just stands there glaring at me, so I go on. "Now as I said before, I believe it essential that we share what we know. Who has responded to your appeal, for example? What have you learned about your dear mother? Come, sit down."

Instead of coming over to the couch, she flounces out the door. I go and call after her, "And of course you'll want to know the location of your mother's final resting place." This of course brings her back inside.

"Where is her grave?" she asks.

"Now let's play fair," I tell her. "I asked my questions first. Who has been in touch with you concerning your mother's death?"

"Listen, you creep, I have a right to know where my mother is buried."

"Of course you do, but I want us to work on this together. Why are you going to the police?"

"I'm going to ask them why there's never been an investigation into my mother's death."

"I can answer that for you. They'll tell you there's no evidence that she died. That's why we have to team up, pool what we know, and I know quite a lot." This gives her pause. I can see her thinking. Should I believe him or ignore him? I say, very tenderly, "You realized she was dead before I told you, didn't you, Penny Jean? You sensed it. It's what brought you back here from California."

I knew my tenderness would work on her eventually. It always worked on her mother. She levels with me finally, looking me straight in the eye. "It's like a sixth sense," she says quietly. "A girl knows when her mother ceases to exist. I've known it for nine years. I should have come sooner, but I wasn't . . . strong enough." Tears spring into her eyes and she adds, "She saved my life by killing my daddy."

"Don't you think I know that?" I say, and she gets huffy again. More than huffy, she has a regular tantrum, shouting, "Of course you know it. You were hanging around our house every time Daddy was out of town. You gave my mother your gun and showed her how to use it. Did you ever love her, or was it our house and property you were after from the start?"

And with that, she's out the door again. I follow her, calling to her as she's getting into a little car with randy Sandy at the wheel, "Your mother's buried in the city dump, Penny Jean." I can't help laughing. It's probably not a nice thing to say to a damsel in distress, but it's such a great line, and how many times in your life do you get to say it to someone? *Your mother is buried in the city dump*. I can't stop laughing.

Dusty

✦

W HEN I COME TO, I'm lyin' in this room where everything's so white and clean I think I musta died and
went to heaven. But then Ollie appears out of nowhere and
tells me not to sit up because I got tubes running into me, so
then I know I'm not in heaven. I've watched enough *ER* to
know a hospital room when I see one.

Well, as long as I can't sit up or walk around, I figure I
might as well have me a little snooze. So I lie back down and
think about Cal'donie. As I told Ollie more than once,
Cal'donie had a religious streak in her. One time I remember
she got her pitcher on the front page of the *Weekly*, her and
Gertie Ann Hulstrom, because them two were the witnesses
to a very religious thing that happened right here in Staggerford. I'm talking about the time a guy got raised up to
heaven right out of a booth in Crusty's Diner.

This was before we got married, but we was goin' together and she told me all about it. Seems this fella name of
Hap Conlon used to come into Crusty's and drink tea about
every afternoon when Cal'donie and Gertie Ann was on

duty. Well, this one afternoon Cal'donie took his order—tea and a sweet roll, I think she said—and when she come back with it, Hap Conlon, so help me God, was sittin' up about three inches off his seat. He was reading the sports page of some newspaper and never seemed to notice, but Cal'donie said she was spooked. "Come 'ere," she called to Gertie Ann. "Come 'ere and tell me if I'm goin' nuts or if Hap Conlon is risin' up off the ground," and Gertie Ann took one look and screamed her fool head off and went to her knees right there, because Hap Conlon kep' risin' up and by this time he was at least a foot and a half above his seat.

Gertie Ann was the one that put a name to it. She bellered out, "It's the Assumption all over again, it's the Assumption all over again!" and the next time the *Weekly* come out they used those words as their headline over the pitcher of Cal'donie and Gertie Ann standin' by that empty booth, which they've kept roped off ever since because people like to come in and look at it, and now and then somebody'll come in and say a prayer next to it. It's been an overall good thing for Crusty's business.

Cal'donie said the funny thing about it was how Hap Conlon didn't seem to even notice what was goin' on. He just kept readin' away and goin' up higher and higher, and then when his head was just about ready to hit the ceiling, Cal'donie decided to take matters into her own hands and she went and grabbed him by the foot and tried to jerk him back down. But it was weird—ever' time she jerked, there was a jerk from the other end, like somebody was above him tryin' to pull him up, and then suddenly there was this deep booming voice filled the restaurant, and it said, "Let go, damn it," and Cal'donie let go of her end and Hap Conlon disappeared above the ceiling and was never seen again.

According to Cal'donie, this was different than the rapture because he kept his clothes on the whole time. There wasn't no heap of his belongings left behind, except of course his car keys, which were lyin' on the table. Another funny thing about it was that accordin' to Hap's wife he wasn't especially a saintly kind of guy. His main interest in life was baseball—she called him "a baseball nut"—and he only went to church four or five times a year, yet he was raised up to heaven, as Cal'donie said, "just like the Lord almighty."

There was such a hullaballoo about it that the Catholic bishop of Berrington come into Crusty's about a week later and asked Cal'donie to go over it with him, and he had a notebook and wrote down every word she said. When she got to the part about the voice that said "Let go, damn it," he was real impressed. He said, "Do you realize there's a chance that it was God Himself speaking to you?" And Cal'donie said, "It wouldn't surprise me none, in Crusty's you meet 'em all."

Ollie

❖

MY UNCLE DUSTY'S IN THE Intensive Care Unit up on the third floor of Mercy Hospital. Except for the ten minutes it took me to go down to the cafeteria in the basement and eat a tuna fish sandwich, I've been with him almost two hours. Seemed to me he was doing a little better for a while—opening his eyes more often and looking confused rather than just lying here in a kind of agitated coma, but Doc Hammond still isn't real optimistic. Although he won't know for sure until he sees the results of the blood test, Doc says he suspects a lot of heart damage. Dusty's got an oxygen mask over his face, along with an IV in his left arm and a heart catheter that goes in under his collarbone. Doc says I should get ready for the worst. He says he's seen cases like Dusty's before and most of them were gone within twenty-four hours.

So I sit here with a pad and pen, composing his eulogy. I suppose if Caledonia were still alive I'd be saving myself the trouble—Caledonia, being a higher-toned person than Dusty, would have had him buried from one of our mainline churches—but now I'm his closest living kin, and I expect it'll be up to me to conduct the service in the local funeral parlor. Dusty was my father's brother, the son of a dirt farmer (my grandfather Luuya) who never made enough money to properly feed and clothe his family, and both boys struck out early to seek their fortune in garbage. They were partners for a time, but they split up because Dusty, my father claimed, was too stupid to remember his garbage route. You can say what you want about Caledonia—you can say she was frumpy and nosy and difficult to get along with—but it's hard to imagine Dusty continuing in the business without her to take him in hand and see that he was prompt and clean and careful with people's garbage cans. My dad went into used car sales after they split up and made a decent living until he got sick and died of lung cancer at the age of fifty-four. My dad, like his brother, was a gentle, passive sort of guy until he had one of his spells of anger. Why I remember one time . . .

But this is more about Dusty's wife and brother than about Dusty himself. I'm having a devil of a time jotting down notes about his life now that I know what he did to Mrs. Nichols. He claims it wasn't his fault because she hit him first, but homicide is homicide and I'm worried about his eternal soul. And what about Caledonia's theory concerning the murder of Mr. Nichols in front of the Paramount?

The first thing I've got to do is verify his story. To do this, I put away my pen and paper and I leave Dusty in the care of the nurses and go downtown to the Chamber of Commerce office to see Susie Nesbitt. Every year Susie is at the Paramount when the Christmas show is on because the

Chamber sponsors it. She must have been there when Mr. Nichols was shot. Besides, she keeps a scrapbook of every article about the Chamber that appears in the *Weekly*. In amongst all her clippings she must have the news about the shooting.

Susie's job consists of sitting at a low desk and staring at a computer screen all day. She puts up a fuss as usual when I show up, acts like it'll kill her to do anybody a favor, but I tell her it's a matter of life and death, and that does it. Her curiosity gets the better of her.

She brings her scrapbooks out of a cabinet and we find the article all right. The newsprint has turned yellow but it's all there, about how Mr. Nichols was shot in the chest with a twenty-two-caliber bullet. I try to turn the pages to follow the investigation, but Susie slams the scrapbook shut, saying, "Tell me what's going on, what you're looking for."

"My uncle Dusty told a story this morning which, if it's true, might explain what happened to the Nichols family."

"So what happened?"

"I can't tell you, it's a secret. I'll tell you after my uncle dies."

"No, tell me now. I won't tell a soul."

"The heck you won't, you'll tell everybody in town. You'll have it printed in the paper."

She knows this is true—gossip is Susie's drug of choice—but she blows her stack anyway. "All right, big boy—out! Get out!"

"Susie, all I'm asking is two more minutes in this scrapbook."

"It's about Needy Nichols' murder, isn't it?"

"Don't call him by that stupid name, Susie. He was called Neddy."

"Neddy might have been his name, but Needy was his nature. Don't ask me how I know."

"I'm not interested in how you know. Now let me look." I make a move toward the book but she clutches it to her breast. Her high-strung, high-pitched voice gives me a headache.

"I know it's about the shooting," she says, "because the rest of the Nichols mystery's been solved. I mean everybody knows what happened to the wife and daughter. The daughter went out West to school and Mrs. Nichols gave her house to her second husband and moved away. Ollie, did you know her second husband's a former Gopher?"

"A what?"

"A Minnesota Gopher. George Bauer played football at the university thirty years ago. And after that he was just your average salesman on the road, until he moved in with Mrs. Nichols on Hillcrest Drive and started living off the fat of the land."

I try once more to grab the book, but it's no use. "All right, Susie, if you must know—do you promise, not a word to anybody?"

Raising her right hand, she says, "Cross my heart."

"My uncle Dusty says Neddy Nichols was shot by his daughter."

"His daughter!" I watch her expression turn sour as she considers this and rejects it. "Your uncle's nuts."

"Okay, okay, let's check it out." She allows me to open the scrapbook.

"It was a stray bullet," says Susie. "Nobody ever found a gun."

"I just want to know if the daughter was at the scene."

"Oh, she was there all right. I saw her."

"You saw her?

"Sure, I was in the lobby. After the kids were gone and the lobby was empty, the Nichols girl came in the door and ran into the auditorium and down the aisle and out the back exit. I didn't know anything about her daddy being shot or I'd've consoled her."

I find the newspaper photo of the scene—a photographer happened to be there to take a picture of the kids swarming outside the theater. There's Mrs. Nichols going to her knees next to her husband's body and, sure enough, there's Penny Jean. She's opening the door to the lobby and she's got her right hand stuffed in a big purse hanging from her shoulder.

"Look here, Susie, she's got this big floppy shoulder bag, so don't you see? That's where the revolver is. My uncle was right, she dropped it into her purse and they later found it in the garbage."

"Who found it?"

"Dusty and Caledonia. It's the gun they used to shoot rats with at the dump."

"So it's true," says Susie, finally convinced. "Penny Jean Nichols and her mother killed her father." She looks awestruck by the truth.

"But you know what stumps me? The motive. Why would a girl want to kill her own daddy?"

"Ollie, don't be stupid. Needy Nichols was pretty weird sexually."

I hate to believe this but maybe it's true. And now I want to check out Dusty's story about Blanche. "What have you got on Mrs. Nichols, her disappearance?"

"Why?" says Susie, slamming the book shut again. "I suppose your uncle's got a theory about her, too?"

"He's under the impression he killed her."

"Who's 'he'?"

"Uncle Dusty."

This shocks her. "Why? What did he have against Mrs. Nichols?"

"She attacked him with a broom handle."

"Oh, go on."

"It's true, she broke his ribs—it's a long story. Let me see the book."

While I page through it, Susie picks up the phone, punches three numbers, and says, "Hello, nine-one-one? I want to report a couple of murders."

I grab the receiver out of her hand. "What are you doing? You promised you wouldn't say anything."

"I promised not to spread gossip. This isn't gossip, this is murder. Now give me the phone."

She tries to wrestle it out of my hand, but I hold on tight. "Now look here, Susie, I know what you're thinking. Dusty committed murder and he owes a debt to society. But in this case—"

"It's what any normal person would think."

"But Dusty's in the hospital. Dr. Hammond says his condition is grave. His heart's just a little flicker on the monitor—I saw it."

She keeps trying to twist the receiver away from me. She

says, "So your uncle's sick. Let the authorities decide what to do. I refuse to be responsible for letting him off the hook."

"Susie, you promised to keep your big mouth shut."

"Listen, for nine years the world's been wondering who shot Needy Nichols and what happened to his wife. I owe the world an explanation."

I give up and release the phone. "Okay, okay, tell the world, but wait till Dusty's dead, will you?"

"No, your uncle's not all there. He needs to be reminded he's a murderer. He's probably forgotten about it."

"All the more reason to let sleeping dogs lie."

"He needs to be told he did wrong!"

"All right, I'll tell him. But you know, Susie, he needs something else a lot more than he needs that."

"Oh, yeah? What?" She's about to dial 911 again.

"He needs to be baptized."

This stops her. "Baptized!" she shrieks. "You're out of your gourd."

She probably isn't worth an explanation, but I explain anyhow. There's always a chance the word of God will sink in. "Susie, Dusty's at the door of death. He's committed this big sin, and he's about to spend eternity being punished for it."

"Good God, Ollie, haven't you heard? There is no hell anymore. The fire in hell went out with the Latin mass. Where have you been?"

"I'm not talking about hellfire. I'm talking about being marked for all eternity as a murderer. Dusty will be an outcast in heaven."

"And what will baptism do for him?"

"All the sins of his life will be swept away. He zips right off to heaven with a clean slate."

"God, you sound just like Sister Angeline."

"Will you come with me, Susie? Help me?"

She laughs as if my invitation is preposterous. "And leave the office? Ollie, are you out of your mind? How could I possibly help you?"

"Dusty needs a godmother."

Her laugh turns into a hysterical shriek, but I keep my cool. "Remember what Sister Angeline used to say: 'It's vanity to think only of this life and not of the life to come.' "

"Poppycock," says Susie, proving herself to be a nonbeliever.

I ask her, "What are you, an atheist?"

"I'm a skeptic," she says, picking up the phone and punching three numbers again. Going out the door, I hear her say for my benefit, I'm sure, "Is this nine-one-one? . . . Prove it!"

Grover

✣

I'M MAKING MY WAY ACROSS the lobby with a sack containing my Whopper and fries when Ollie comes running in all excited, telling me, "Hey Grover, grab your coat, we haven't got a minute to lose. We gotta go to the hospital and baptize Dusty."

This kind of foolish talk doesn't deserve a response. I sit down in my easy chair and take out my Whopper.

Waving a small, leatherbound prayer book in his hand, he says, "My uncle needs to be baptized so he'll be comfortable in heaven. We pour a little water, say a little prayer, and bingo!—his murder rap is down the drain. Take my word for it, Grover, I'd do the same for you."

"Like hell you would—over my dead body." They didn't put any pickles on my Whopper.

"Look," he says, "we'll have to take some stuff with us." He finds a page in his prayer book. "Okay, here we are. 'Baptism Adult.' " He reads to himself for a minute. "Uh-oh, adult baptism involves instruction in the faith, conversion of life, all kinds of things Dusty won't have time for. We'd better go with infant baptism, it's a lot simpler."

"You just go on ahead without me," I tell him. It makes me mad when they forget pickles.

"I can't do it alone," says Ollie. "It'll take one of us to do it and the other one to be godfather. Besides, this is probably your last chance to see my uncle Dusty alive. Susie Nesbitt's calling the cops on him and if he isn't dead by morning he'll be in jail."

"Dead?" I'm shocked. Dusty's been having about one heart attack per week as long as I can remember.

"Doc Hammond doesn't expect him to last twenty-four hours."

"Criminey, why didn't you say so—Dusty's behind in his room rent."

I go for my coat.

Ollie checks his prayer book. "We'll need holy water, holy oil, and holy salt." He digs around in my Whopper bag and takes out a little paper envelope of salt, and then he picks my bottle of mineral water off the counter. "Water and salt," he says, proudly.

"They ain't holy," I tell him.

"Just wait, they will be," he says. "Come on, there's a can of motor oil in my car."

Ollie's car is a fifteen-year-old Ford with muffler trouble. We sound like a tractor in cold weather, and it's plenty cold out today. I hate the thought of another winter coming. When we get within two or three blocks of Mercy Hospital, he turns off to the right.

"Hey, where we going?"

"Lucky for us, Father Mittleholtz is still living in St. Isidore's rectory," says Ollie.

"Father Mittleholtz! He's senile."

"I know, but he's still good for a blessing or two. In his heyday he was always a great one for blessing things. Why I remember one time, on the Feast of St. Isidore the Farmer, he came outside after mass and blessed a whole truckload of pigs."

There's a circle drive leading up to the front of St. Isidore's rectory, and instead of parking in the street like I would've done, Ollie pulls right up next to the front door. "Wait here," he tells me, "I'll see if he's home."

He gets out and rings the doorbell. A young priest comes to the door, and I roll down my window so I can hear their conversation.

"Hello, Father," says Ollie. "I was just wondering if Father Mittleholtz is home this afternoon."

The priest gives Ollie a curious look, as if nobody's asked for the old guy in years. "Sorry," he says, "Father Mittleholtz is having his lunch."

"Well, what I was wondering, do you suppose he could just step out here a minute and bless my car?"

"Bless your car?" The priest obviously thinks Ollie is nuts.

"Yeah, you know, his routine blessing for cars and bikes and pigs. See, my car is so old and the tires are so bald I'm afraid I'll have an accident." The priest doesn't budge, so Ollie introduces himself. "Gosh, I'm sorry," he says, "I never told you who I am. The Reverend Ollie Luuya, very pleased to meet you."

This is getting too embarrassing for me. I roll up my window so I don't hear what else they say—and besides, there's a cold wind blowing down my neck—and pretty soon the young priest comes out and stands in front of the car and waves his hand over the hood ornament, and Ollie says, "Thanks a million, praise the Lord," and he gets in behind the wheel and we drive away. Ollie's real happy and pleased with himself. He says to me, "We just got the car blessed along with everything in it—the oil, the water, and the salt."

I tell him, "That's a dang funny religion them Catholics got."

"And you, yourself, Grover, you got blessed along with everything else."

"I wouldn't be too sure. I ducked out of the way when he waved his hand."

"Oh, you know what the Bible says about that. *Thou canst not duck from the Lord.* Paul's letter to the Thisselonians, chapter three."

At the hospital he drives around to the back and pulls into staff parking. "Hey, what are we doing back here?" I ask him. "This is where the doctors and nurses go in."

"We don't want to attract attention with this oil," he says, reaching into the backseat and handing me a can of thirty-weight Pennzoil. "I got the water and salt," he says. "Come on."

By the time we climb up the back stairway to the third floor, I'm tuckered out. I follow Ollie into a room with two beds, but only one of them occupied. It's Dusty lying there sleeping. I don't know him at first without his cap and overalls on. He's covered with a sheet and there's a tube leading to an oxygen mask on his face. He's pale as paper.

"Hey, Dusty," I tell him real jollylike, but he doesn't seem to hear me. I tell Ollie, "Your uncle don't look so hot."

"Never mind," says Ollie. "He must be improving—this morning they had more tubes running into him." Ollie's all business. He hands me a can opener and tells me to open the oil, which I do, and he gets right to work. He reads out loud from his prayer book, *"The priest breathes gently three times upon the face of the infant."* He leans over Dusty and says between breaths, *"Depart from Uncle Dusty, thou unclean spirit. . . . And give place to the Holy Ghost the Paraclete."* Then, reading ahead, he says, "Uh-oh, I'm going to need both hands. Hold the book for me, would you, Grover?"

I hold it up in front of his face and he reads, *"The priest then makes, with his thumb, the sign of the cross on the infant's lips and breast while placing his other hand on the infant's head."*

At his touch, Dusty wakes up. He blinks a few times and says, "Hey, what's going on? What are you guys doing here?"

"Your rent's overdue," I tell him.

Ollie says, "Just lie still and relax, Dusty. You're getting baptized."

He struggles to raise himself on his elbows. "Baptized!"

"You won't be sorry," says Ollie. "Just take my word for it."

"Who says I'm sorry," says Dusty. "Heck, one thing Cal'donie always wanted was for me to get baptized. Cal'donie had religion, you remember that, Grover."

While I get his attention, I tell him, "It comes to twenty-two fifty, what you owe on your room."

"Next he puts a little of the blessed salt in the mouth of

the babe saying, 'Receive the salt of wisdom, may it be to thee a propitiation unto everlasting life.' " When he does this, Dusty spits, but it doesn't faze Ollie. He says to me, "Say 'Amen,' Grover."

"Amen," says I.

"Peace be with you. Say, 'And with thy spirit,' Grover."

"And with thy spirit," says I.

"She tried out the different ones," says Dusty, speaking of Caledonia. "She was born and raised in the North Dakota synod of the Screamin' Meemies, or some such domination. But she was Baptist when I married her. She even went over to the Catholics for a while, but she got turned off Catholics the time a bunch of 'em invited her along on a bus ride to see the pope o' Rome." He lifts the oxygen mask off his mouth to say this, then he clamps it back on for a few swigs of good air.

Ollie tries to keep him silent by saying, "Hey, Dusty, would you save it till later? We gotta get this over with," but of course there's no shutting Dusty up when he gets going on Caledonia.

"She got herself all gussied up to meet the pope o' Rome. This was years ago. She got her hair fixed and bought a new dress. Why she even studied how to say 'Hi' and 'Good-bye' and 'How's your honor doin' today,' in French or Ethiopian or whatever it is the pope talks in, and they went clear to Ioway on a school bus." He pauses to suck more air.

"Dusty, your heart," says Ollie.

"Never mind," I tell him. "Once you get him started you'll never stop him."

Ollie then points to a computer screen over the head of the bed, which I'd noticed but never paid any attention to.

"That's his heart," he says, and sure enough you can see this green line going up and down for a few beats, and then it'll get all scrambly for a bit and then go back to up and down.

"She told me she felt like she was bein' carried off by aliens because everybody took out their rosary beads and started in recitin' Hail Marys as if their life depended on it. And it wasn't only the rosary beads, it was the heat. The air conditioning went kaflooey and by the time they got down south o' Minneapolis it was ninety-five degrees with the sun shinin' right in on Cal'donie because she was settin' in the front seat because she always got bilious settin' in back.

"And then come the last straw. Here they been goin' bumpity bumpity bumpity for three hundred miles and where does it get 'em? It gets 'em to Ioway. *'Ioway!'* she says to the bus driver, 'I know the pope o' Rome don't live in Minnesota, but this is ridiculous.' "

He sinks back to suck more air and to let his heart settle down, and this gives Ollie a chance to get in a few more licks. He reads, *"He then takes the holy oil on his thumb and anoints the infant upon the breast and between the shoulder blades saying, 'I anoint thee with the oil of salvation, that thou mayst have life everlasting.'* Say 'Amen,' Grover."

"Amen," says I.

"Hey, that tickles," says Dusty when he feels Ollie's oily thumb on his chest.

"Can't be helped," says Ollie. "It's your ticket to paradise."

Dusty gathers his strength for a final push. "Then comes the *real* last straw. The bus pulls into a stubblefield full of about a thousand other buses, and Cal'donie gets up on her high horse and says, 'I come along to see the pope o' Rome, not attend no bus convention,' and the bus driver says to her, 'Well, you come to the right place, honey, there he is,' and he points to a teeny, tiny speck up on a platform half a mile away. 'Well, I'll be dipped in shit,' says Cal'donie, 'the pope o' Rome ain't no bigger than a flyspeck.' And pretty soon she hears some organ music and everybody starts singin' 'On Top of Old Smokey,' or some such hymn and some other specks join the pope on the platform and they go through some falderol, and Cal'donie falls asleep, and before you know it the bus is pullin' outa the stubblefield and headin' for home. Well, that's her last day as a Catholic. She goes back and rejoins the Baptists the next Sunday. She says never mind if they ain't got bingo, the Baptists will never pull a fast one on you like takin' you clear to Ioway to meet the pope o' Rome.'"

That's the end of his story. He sinks back, exhausted, and clamps the mask over his face as Ollie gets out his water bottle and says, "Okay, Uncle Dusty, it's time for the water of life." He splashes water over Dusty's head and shoulders and Dusty sputters, but he's too weak to do anything about it, so he just keeps lying there. His heart line is all squiggly on the monitor. Then Ollie says to me, "Hey, Grover, help me get him over on his stomach, I forgot to anoint his back."

As we struggle to turn him over, his oxygen tube comes loose and the mask drops to the floor. "Hey, you guys, I can't breathe," he says.

I drop down on my knees looking for it, while Ollie tries to reassure him. "This'll just take a second, Dusty. The book says I gotta anoint you between the shoulder blades."

"I can't breathe," Dusty says again.

"That's fine, I'm finished," says Ollie. "Now you can roll over on your back, Dusty. Put the mask back on his face, Grover."

I can't find it. I'm under the bed looking for it when this high-pitched, sirenlike noise starts coming out of the monitor. I saw this happen on TV often enough—it's the sound your heart makes in a hospital when it stops beating. "Hey, Ollie, his heart!" says I.

"I know," says Ollie. "Quick, somebody's coming."

We skedaddle over and crouch down behind the other bed. It's two people in white. The woman's got one of those cute little nurse's caps on her head, and the man's a big bruiser—six two anyway, and built real strong. They turn off the siren—Dusty's heartbeat is a straight, dead line—and they work him over for about half a minute, then they give up and straighten out his body and draw the sheet up over his face.

"Go find Dr. Hammond," says the nurse. "I'll call down to the morgue." They both leave the room.

I start to stand up, but Ollie grabs me by the coat and pulls me down behind the bed again. Somebody else comes in. It's George Bauer, of all people. He shuts the door and goes straight over to the bed. He takes the pillow from under Dusty's head and kneels on the bed and presses the pillow on Dusty's face with all his might for a full half a minute. Then he leans down and puts his ear to Dusty's chest and listens for life signs. Then he notices the monitor, the straight green line. He thinks he's killed Dusty and he busts out laughing like a maniac. He presses down on the pillow once again to make sure, and that's when the door opens and in comes the big guy in white with Dr. Hammond.

"Hey, what's going on? What are you doing here?" they shout, and they grab George Bauer and haul him out of the room. We wait a minute, then we follow them out skedaddle down the stairs and out to Ollie's car, and we make it back to the hotel safe and sound. Of course, my Whopper's stone cold.

Ollie

✦

GROVER AND I GET BACK to the hotel at the same time Penny Jean and her companion do. It turns out her companion *is* her husband—at least that's how she introduces him. He's a short, husky, broad-shouldered guy named Sandy Sanderson. He gives us both a tighter handshake than necessary—I notice Grover cringe. Grover says to him, "You don't look too shabby for a man that just had his nose broke."

"You saw that bastard hit me?"

"Sure, I was here at the counter, minding the hotel."

"He gave me a bloody nose," says Sandy, "but he never broke it."

"He's the creep that took over my mother's property after she disappeared," says Penny Jean.

I explain what we know, which is quite a little when you consider what Dusty told us and what happened at the hospital. When I get to the part about Dusty's vision of how her mother died, Penny Jean gets real agitated. "Yes, yes!" she says, jumping up and down. "That was no vision. I always

wondered if George Bauer did away with her. It makes perfect sense."

"And he was an accomplice in your dad's murder, too," I
tell her. "Grover heard you say he planned it with you before
you shot him."

"No, no, it wasn't me!" She gives me a desperate look.

"Well, I thought since Susie Nesbitt saw you running
through the theater with your hand in your shoulder bag,
that you had the revolver with you."

"I did. I had it in my purse. But I didn't fire it."

"Then who did?"

"My mother, because my dad . . . well, let's just say he
was doing evil stuff, and George Bauer helped us plan how
to go about it." She doesn't seem to have the least trouble
spilling out the story cool as you please. "See, my mother
shot him in the chest and dropped the gun into my purse
and I ran through the theater and out the fire exit and went
home and threw it in the garbage. And the next day I was
on a plane to California."

"The Dell Rapids Clinic," says Grover, proud to show how
much he knows about it.

Penny Jean nods. "But we didn't call it a clinic at first. It
was called the Dell Rapids Dude Ranch and Spa. It's all part
of the same operation."

"So you were sent out there under false pretenses."

"No . . . well, in a way, I guess. I mean I didn't plan on
spending years of my life there. I guess my mother probably
knew I'd flip out when I heard that she married George
Bauer. I hated that rat, and still do." At this point she breaks
down. She drops into Dusty's chair and her eyes fill with

tears. "And now from what you say, it was George Bauer who killed her. I always thought so."

Grover says, "Hold your horses, young lady, we never said George Bauer killed her."

"But he said the garbageman . . ." She points at me.

"What he said was the garbageman *imagined* George Bauer killed her, imagined George Bauer dropped a rock on her head. We can show you the rock. Dusty keeps it in his room." Grover looks around the lobby, and says something very scary: "Where the heck *is* Dusty?" The first signs of forgetfulness or dementia always scare the heck out of me, because it's like the victim is entering another world and leaving me behind.

Penny Jean says, "But he didn't imagine it, don't you see? He actually saw it. George Bauer never really loved my mother. He married her for her money and her Hillcrest property, and then he did away with her."

"Hey, you guys, did you hear?" Here comes Susie Nesbitt, rushing into the lobby like the town crier she is and shattering our peaceful little conversation. "George Bauer's in jail!"

"We know all about it," I tell her.

"But just wait till you hear why. Somebody caught him at the hospital trying to *off* somebody."

"We know that, too," I tell her.

"You know? How can you possibly know?" she screeches. "I only heard it myself five minutes ago." Then she notices Penny Jean sitting in Dusty's chair, and a look of terror crosses her face as she says to me, "Who's your girlfriend, Ollie?"

This is when Grover gets out of his chair and leaves the

room. He can't stand Susie Nesbitt—she's too high-strung for Grover. He beckons to Sandy Sanderson on his way upstairs and Sandy follows him.

"Susie Nesbitt," I say, "meet Mrs. Sanderson."

She gives Penny Jean a curt nod and says, "Pleasure, I'm sure." Then she gives me this seething look and says, "Ollie, what's she *doing* here?"

"She's staying here."

This really tees her off. "How long has this been going on?"

Penny Jean speaks up and cools her down by saying, "Look, what's your problem? I'm in town to find out what became of my mother. My husband and I are leaving this weekend—if that will make you happy."

This softens Susie considerably. She pats Penny Jean on the shoulder and says, "So you're the Nichols girl—why didn't you say so? You remember me, surely. I'm Susie Nesbitt."

Penny Jean says she's sorry, she doesn't remember.

"But of course you do. I was your dad's right hand in those days. I remember the day you killed him like it was yesterday." There's an embarrassed silence. Susie says, "What's the matter? Did I say something wrong?"

I expect Penny Jean to answer her, but she doesn't. So I do. "She didn't kill her father."

Susie shrieks, "Then who did, for God's sake? This morning you said Penny Jean shot him in the heart."

"That was this morning. Since then we've learned a few things." I explain to her about the murder, about Penny Jean disposing of the gun, about the whole deal, but Susie doesn't look convinced. She says, "Who told you that?"

"Penny Jean and my uncle."

"Your uncle!"

"He was their garbageman—it's a long story."

Still she looks suspicious. I can practically see the gears turning in her brain. She's wondering if Penny Jean told us the truth. This gets me to wondering the same thing.

This is when Grover comes downstairs followed by Sandy Sanderson, who's carrying Dusty's rock. It's a big one—it must weigh forty pounds. Dusty always kept it on the floor and used it as a doorjamb when it was hot and he needed a breeze through his room.

"Hey, where you going with my uncle's rock?" I ask.

Grover says, "It's the rock Dusty picked up from beside Mrs. Nichols."

He clears a place for the rock on the counter, between his registration book and his cell phone. "I figure if Penny Jean is right about who killed her mother," he says, "then maybe George Bauer's fingerprints are still on it."

Grover is shrewder than I've given him credit for.

He goes on. "Dusty keeps the twenty-two revolver in his underwear drawer, but it's no use looking there for fingerprints. It's been used by Dusty and Caledonia since the murder."

"Now we're getting somewhere," says Penny Jean, and she jumps up from the chair and throws her arms around Grover, planting a wet kiss on his cheek.

Grover

✤

WE ALL STAND AROUND staring at the rock like a bunch of fools, as if it's going to show us a set of fingerprints of its own accord. Then Penny Jean reaches for my cordless. She punches in a number she knows by heart—seven digits, so at least it's a free call, not long distance. She gets somebody on the line named Len. It's Len Morehouse, our chief of police. You've got to hand it to this little stick of dynamite, she's a go-getter. First thing she did after George Bauer left the hotel, she got the police to look for her mother's body in the dumpgrounds. And now she explains all about the rock that we've got here on the counter, and she tells Len—doesn't ask him—to look it over for George Bauer's fingerprints. She listens to Len's response for a minute and then slams down the phone in disgust.

"Your local cop says he'd never find fingerprints on a rock unless it's real smooth. Besides, he says, what would it prove? It wouldn't prove George Bauer used it to kill my mother."

Olllie's got the answer. "Yes it would," he says, "if there's still a trace of your mother's blood on it."

We examine it all over, rolling it back and forth over the counter, but the streak of red Dusty said was on it must've got worn off. There's no sign of it.

We're all feeling pretty downcast when Susie Nesbitt comes up with this idea. She says, "If you've got George Bauer's revolver upstairs, we can pin Mr. Nichols' murder on him. I mean ballistics will prove the bullet came from that gun." It isn't a bad idea, but I wish Susie wouldn't have to screech like the whistle of a freight train every time she says something.

"But how do we prove it belonged to George Bauer?" says Penny Jean. "Nobody had to register guns back in those days."

This takes the wind out of Susie's sails. She gives Penny Jean a disgusted look, as if she'd like to kill her.

Ollie's got another idea. He says, "So we put him away for killing Dusty. I mean the doctor and the orderly saw him kneeling on his chest and smothering him with a pillow."

Then it all comes back to me, where Dusty is. I keep forgetting he's dead. Then it occurs to me that Ollie hasn't got such a great idea after all. "You can't convict somebody for killing a dead man," says I. "The doctor and the orderly knew Dusty was dead before George Bauer showed up. That's what bothers me about the whole deal, Ollie. You and me—we killed him."

I get this horrified look from everybody, including Ollie, who says, "Don't say that, Grover, it's not true."

"It's the God's truth. We went in the room he was alive, we came out he was dead."

"He died on our watch, I'll grant you. But we weren't responsible."

"Heck we weren't. We took his air away from him, and that's what he died of. Lack of air, plain and simple."

Ollie gets pretty excited. "Grover, don't you ever say that again! Don't you realize you could get us put in jail for life?" He explains to the others, "All that happened was that Dusty's oxygen mask fell off while we were baptizing him."

"Baptizing him!" shrieks Susie Nesbitt. "You mean you actually went ahead and baptized him?"

"We sure did, didn't we, Grover? The last word out of my uncle Dusty's mouth was 'Amen.'"

His last word was "I can't breathe," but I don't remind Ollie. He's got this absolutely blissful look in his eye that means he's imagining heaven. He's saying, "This very minute Dusty's reunited with his beloved Caledonia in paradise." Why don't more Christian believers commit suicide, is what I'd like to know. I mean, if heaven is such a wonderful paradise, why aren't people like Ollie more eager to get there? I don't ask him, because instead of a straight answer, he'd quote from Paul's letter to the Collisions or some such text, and I've heard enough of that stuff to last me the rest of my life.

Sandy Sanderson pipes up then and says if we can't convict George Bauer for murdering Dusty, how about getting him for attempted murder, which is the craziest idea so far, but the four of them chew it over, discussing the pros and cons, until I've heard all I can stand. I call up my cousin Henry's boy and ask him to come over and settle us down. My cousin's boy, Henry Junior, is a lawyer. He's got an office down the street. He's Johnny-on-the-spot, and tells me he'll be right over.

Henry Junior

❧

I'VE BEEN LOOKING FOR an excuse to leave the office early anyway, so I drop in on Cousin Grover and his goofy preacher friend Ollie Luuya. All Grover said on the phone was that he needed an argument settled, so I thought it'd be something about the daily mean temperature over the last forty years or some such foolishness. But when I get there I find they're talking about murder, and not hypothetically. They've got the Nichols girl staying there and they've taken up the case of her father's killing and her mother's disappearance. The Nichols girl is now named Penny Jean Sanderson and she has her husband from California along with her. He's a quiet guy, built like a linebacker, only shorter. And Susie Nesbitt is also there of course, because she can smell out gossip from clear down the street at the Chamber office, where she works.

The Sandersons don't say much and even Susie Nesbitt keeps her mouth shut while Cousin Grover and Ollie tell me what they know. It seems Ollie's uncle the garbageman, who died this afternoon in Mercy Hospital, thought he saw George Bauer kill Blanche Nichols by dropping a rock on her head, only she wasn't Blanche Nichols anymore—she was Blanche Bauer, because by the time she died she was married to her alleged murderer. This happened nine years ago. There's a rock on the registration counter they claim is the weapon he used. Ollie's in a sweat to get George Bauer convicted of murder. The Sandersons are, too. I figure the Sandersons want George Bauer's property because he got it through treachery. Or so they seem to think.

"How about you?" I ask Susie Nesbitt because she's sitting there with a skeptical look on her face.

"I don't believe it," she says. "I mean, how can you convict a guy of murder if nobody saw him do it except some dimwit who thought he only imagined it."

"Oh, he saw it all right," says Ollie. "The only trouble was he was sitting in his garbage truck and he saw it happen though a mirror. Dusty was always confused by mirrors. Unless he could look at a thing straight on, he always suspected it wasn't true. But we've got the rock here to prove it," he says.

"The rock doesn't prove a thing," I tell him. "It would take a miracle to get fingerprints off that rock, and if you did, it would only prove that a lot of different people had handled the thing in the last nine years."

"But it might still have Mrs. Nichols' blood on it," says Ollie.

"It's no good, I tell you. Even if you found blood, it wouldn't prove who dropped it on her head. Look, forget it. A dead man's testimony repeated by his friends won't stand up in court. The county attorney'd have to be nuts to prosecute a case like that."

Penny Jean Sanderson then pipes up. "Say, you know what? George Bauer had his name engraved on his revolver!" She looks like she just discovered gold, but I don't get it, so she explains that her mother shot her father at George Bauer's prompting and with George Bauer's revolver. She says that since he was an accomplice and her mother's dead, we ought to pin her father's killing on him.

"Now wait a minute," I say. "You mean your father was murdered by your mother?"

She admits it. She says her father had been sexually abusing her and when her mother found out, she and George Bauer planned how to go about killing him. Penny Jean says she remembers seeing Bauer's name on the gun before she threw it in the garbage. She says her mother handed it to her at the murder scene and she took it home. The gun's now upstairs in Dusty Luuya's room, because he found it in the garbage and used it for killing rats at the dump. The name is engraved on the barrel. She says ballistics will prove the bullet came from his gun.

I don't tell her how stupid this is. I tell her I see a lot of problems with it. First of all, where's the bullet? If it's still lodged in Neddy Nichols' heart, his body will have to be disinterred, and if it's not, where is it? Second, even if the gun proves to be the murder weapon, there's no proof that George Bauer fired it. "Which brings me to the biggest problem of all—you can't go to court and try to convict a man of a crime he didn't commit."

"Why not?" says Penny Jean. "If we can't convict him of the crime he *did* commit . . ."

Susie Nesbitt pipes up then and says, "But he was an accomplice to murder. At least you can convict him of that."

I point out that Penny Jean was an accomplice as well. "You don't want to risk getting her in hot water."

"Oh, she was only a child."

"Right, I was only a child," says Penny Jean. "Besides, we don't have to bring me into it at all."

"But of course you do. If you're using the revolver as proof, you're going to have to tell the court where it's been these past nine years. And you're going to have to admit your part in the scheme."

Penny Jean starts looking pretty desperate when I add that the whole bunch of them could all be convicted of perjury for trying to pin a murder on a man who didn't commit it. She cries out, "My mother's in the city dump! Somebody's got to pay for that!"

Her mother in the city dump is news to me. Ollie explains how his uncle Dusty, thinking that he himself killed Mrs. Nichols, threw her body out with the garbage. He says the authorities have been out there since noon today, trying to dig her up.

"So why did Dusty think he killed her?" I ask.

"Because he struck her with his fist," says Ollie, "after she broke his ribs."

"Broke his ribs?" says Penny Jean. "You never told me that."

I ask, "You mean Mrs. Nichols had a fight with her garbageman?" This gets more preposterous by the minute.

"She happened to be outside when Dusty stopped at her house," says Ollie. "And he said something to her that roused her to anger or desperation or something. Anyhow she came at him with her broom handle and broke a couple of ribs."

"What did he say to her?"

"I don't remember offhand. Grover, what did Dusty say to Mrs. Nichols?"

Grover says, "Something about the weather I suppose. He was usually interested in the weather."

"No, no, he said something that got her all steamed up, remember?"

Grover doesn't respond to this. He sits there motionless, like he's in a coma, except his eyes are open and they're fixed on the rock on the counter. Ollie tries to stir him up. He says, "Come on, get with the program, Grover. Remember what happened to the brides in the Bible when they fell asleep at the switch—the bridegrooms passed them by. Now I'm asking you what Dusty said to Mrs. Nichols the morning he buried her in the city dump."

At this point Old Lady Heffington, who owns the hotel, comes in and calls Grover over to a corner to talk to her.

The shrill voice of Susie Nesbitt: "It isn't called a 'dump' anymore, Ollie! It's been called a 'landfill' for at least ten years."

The weepy voice of Penny Jean: "My mother was not an aggressive person."

"Not aggressive!" I say, and I stop there. She's breaking down, so I don't point out to her that murder is a pretty aggressive act. Instead, I tell everybody to calm down. "Never mind what the garbageman said to Mrs. Nichols. Do you know what I think? It sounds to me like the garbageman is the guilty party."

"No, he *thought* he was the guilty party," says Ollie, "but then he climbed into his truck and saw, through his mirror, Mrs. Nichols start to get to her feet and George Bauer approach with this rock and finish her off with it."

"Where was she, in the garbage truck?" Susie wants to know.

"No, she was lying in her yard near the alley, near the back end of the truck."

"If Dusty was in his truck," says Susie, "he was obviously about to run away." Susie likes to play the devil's advocate.

"No, he was trying to think," says Ollie. "We all know my uncle Dusty didn't have the swiftest brain in town. He said, because he didn't have his wife along that day—Caledonia used to tell him every move to make—he needed to climb up behind the wheel and figure out what to do next."

By the time I leave the hotel, they're trying to figure out how to pin Dusty Luuya's death on George Bauer, even though Dusty was dead when Bauer came in and smothered him. This is a crazy bunch of people. I'm putting on my coat and going out the door when Ollie calls me back. He says, "I remember what my uncle Dusty said to Mrs. Nichols. He said, 'You better tell George that Penny Jean is coming home or you'll be sorry.'"

"Coming home from where?" I ask.

"From California, where she's been hospitalized. See, it

was called the Dell Rapids Dude Ranch and Spa, but really it was a mental hospital and Penny Jean . . ."

I let the door go shut behind me and step out in the fresh air.

I stop in at the bar in the next block and order a tall drink to clear my head.

Grover

❧

Now I'm living in Florida, with my sister Grace. Ollie Luuya drove me down here. I haven't been in touch with Ollie since the day he dropped me off here at Grace's condo in Coral Gables. He lives in Miami someplace, and he's going great guns as a preacher. I know that from the letters he writes to the *Staggerford Weekly*, which comes to me through the mail. Every few issues he'll have a letter in there about saving your soul, with a reference to some Bible passage or other. Last week, I recall, he was all het up about Paul's letter to the Romanians.

I hated to leave Staggerford, but it wasn't the same around there with Dusty gone, and now the Ransford Hotel is history. I'll never forget the day Old Lady Heffington came in with the bad news. There were a bunch of us hanging around the lobby shooting the breeze—Ollie, Susie Nesbitt, the Nichols girl and her husband from California, my cousin Henry Junior—and the old dame pulled me aside and said she'd sold the hotel to the city, and they were going to tear it down to make a parking lot. She said the wrecking ball was to move in in the spring, late March or early April.

"Don't worry, Grover dear," she said, taking my hand in her cold fingers and patting it gently. "You can work for me at home. I have scads of bedrooms, one of which will be yours, and you can run errands and such." This is the last thing in the world I want to do, but I don't tell her. Instead, I give her hand a little squeeze and say, "Thank you, Mrs. Heffington," as if I'm overwhelmed by her kindness and I send her on her way.

You see, ever since her husband the robber baron died, Mrs. Heffington's been sort of sweet on me. For a long time she'd been stopping by once or twice a week to shoot the breeze and check me out as a potential live-in companion. Ollie used to give me a bad time about this, until I put my foot down. I've never cared to be teased, as Ollie learned the day I told him to back off. I also told him I'd move to Coral Gables where my sister lives before I'd move in with Mrs. Heffington, and that got him interested. He said he'd been considering a change of scene himself because there aren't all that many Bible-thumping churches around Minnesota. He said the South is where he could really go to town preaching repentance and forgiveness. He said all I need to do is just say the word and he'd gas up his old car and off we'll go, heading for Florida.

So that day, after Mrs. Heffington left, I said to Ollie, "It's time." Ollie made a couple of calls canceling himself out of certain preaching engagements, and I called up my sister and told her I was coming down, and a couple of days later, after the Nichols girl and her husband checked out, I locked up the hotel and off we went. I left a note on the door for people who might be looking for a room, and for Mrs. Heffington, so she wouldn't send a posse out looking for me. The note said,

> *Sorry, gone south*
> —the management

There was a layer of snow laying around Minnesota and Wisconsin, but that pretty much disappeared when we got to Illinois and beyond. We drove clear to Paduca the first day, stayed at a motel for three times as much as I ever charged for a room, and got to Tallahassee the next evening. I was all for sleeping in the car because the cost of motels was putting quite a little hole in my savings, but Ollie insisted he had to be fresh the next morning because he was going to visit the seminary he'd graduated from and never seen. It was called the College of God in the Spirit or some such name. He looked through three or four telephone books, and he even went in to the state capitol and asked people, but never found a trace of it. The third day we pulled in here and my sister, whose husband died and left her pretty well fixed, took me in and I've been basking in sunshine all winter.

About once a month I've been getting a letter from Old Lady Heffington. She must've tracked me down by getting my address from the *Weekly* office. I opened the first two because I thought she might be sending me a check for my last month's pay, but no, they were just about how she's keeping that room in her house open for me, so I've thrown the rest away unopened.

The *Weekly*'s been fascinating on the subject of the Nichols' murder case. Penny Jean and her husband returned to Staggerford for the trial, which they lost because there wasn't any proof that George Bauer killed anybody. Henry Junior wasn't involved in that trial, but he soon turned up as the prosecutor in a civil suit that Penny Jean brought up against George Bauer, claiming he cheated her out of property. It all came down to whether Bauer could produce any paper saying he bought or had been given the big house with its two-story deck and its three-car garage, and he couldn't do it, except he's listed on the county tax roles as the owner, and that tied the jury up in knots. It ended in a hung jury. Penny Jean swears she's going to have another go at it as soon as she can afford the legal fees. Meanwhile, George Bauer walks away a free man, and I hate the thought of that. Ever since Ollie and I saw him kneeling on Dusty's chest and pressing a pillow over his face, I've detested that slimy bastard.

Ollie

❖

I NEVER REALIZED how long it takes spring to get to Minnesota until I drove north with Grover. I mean, all through Illinois and southern Wisconsin the leaves are out, while here in Staggerford the trees are bare as winter. On the last leg of our journey, after lunch in the Twin Cities, Grover mutters all the way north, complaining about the cold and the lack of greenery. "We're only back here for a short time," I keep reminding him, but he keeps on saying, "Oh, the palm trees, the ocean, the sand, the sun."

What we're back here for is the third trial of George Bauer. I prayed about it and decided that George Bauer would never be convicted without the testimony of me and Grover. I located Penny Jean Nichols by telephone, and she agreed. It took a superhuman effort on my part to pry Grover out of that slick condo on the beach, but here he is, in the Berrington Courthouse, dressed in his shiny black suit and orange necktie as his first cousin once removed, Henry Grover, Jr., lays out the case against George Bauer.

Henry tells the jury that after Neddy Nichols was mysteriously shot and killed, George Bauer married Mrs. Nichols in order to get the Hillcrest property, then he murdered her so he and his honey, the new Mrs. Bauer, could move in and occupy the house that rightfully belongs to Penny Jean Nichols. Penny Jean's had a makeover since I last saw her. She's blonde now, and with her makeup and her little black dress, she looks fetching. Her husband, Sandy Sanderson, has put on weight. George Bauer, sitting over on the other side of the courtroom and giving everybody his kindliest smile, has shaved his goatee. He's trying to look innocent as a lamb, but he can't cover up his sinister heart. It shows through plain as day.

Grover doesn't have to say much. He's only called upon to verify my story about what my uncle Dusty saw that day at the Nichols house. I don't dress up the story very much. I admit that Dusty knocked Mrs. Nichols down because she broke his ribs with a broomstick. I say that he actually saw George Bauer drop the rock on his wife's head as she lay there in the garden, and this gets me in trouble with the defense attorney, a beefy, bald-headed fellow from Berrington named Donaldson.

"If he saw George Bauer kill his wife, why did he take the body to the landfill?" Donaldson asks me.

This is a very good question, and it takes me a couple of seconds to put my answer together. "Because Dusty didn't believe what he saw," I tell him. "He was sitting in the cab of his truck when it happened and he saw it through his mirror. You see, my uncle was a little on the retarded side and he never believed what he saw through mirrors. So he was under the impression that he himself had killed Mrs. Nichols when he knocked her down."

Then Donaldson asks the question I've been waiting for. "Didn't George Bauer know that Dusty saw him?"

"Of course he did. That's why he tried to kill Dusty in the hospital."

And that's when Henry Junior brings in the nurse and the orderly that caught George Bauer in the act of trying to suffocate Dusty. That clinches it. The jury all turn and look at Bauer with conviction in their eyes. Not that they make easy work of it. The trial lasts all afternoon, and the jury goes out around five p.m. and they don't come back with their verdict until lunchtime the next day. I'm about to hyperventilate when the judge says, "How do you find the defendant?" and the foreman stands up and looks at the judge and says "Guilty, your honor." Pandemonium breaks out in the courtroom. Judging by all the clapping and cheering, I'd say George Bauer doesn't have too many friends around here.

Grover

✦

"**G**UILTY, YOUR HONOR" MUST BE about the sweetest words in the language. Everybody else must think so, too, the way they're hugging and clapping each other on the back. Why, they kick up such a fuss you'd think George Bauer didn't have a friend in the world. His wife, who they say enjoys the heck out of their house on Hillcrest, is probably going to be mad as a hornet. She never showed up at the trial. I overheard somebody say her bowling league was rolling its final game and her team needed her. The judge pounds his gavel for order, but nobody pays any attention until he shouts, "Everybody, shut up!" because the proceedings aren't over— he has to pass sentence yet. Judge McWorter is his name. He's a little guy, sixty or so, with thick glasses. He says he won't stand for any more behavior like this in his courtroom. His eyes roam around the room, staring each of us down, then he passes sentence. He gives George Bauer forty-eight hours to vacate the property on Hillcrest in favor of Penny Jean Sanderson and to pay Penny Jean damages of five thousand dollars, plus all court costs and attorney fees.

"That's it?" cries Penny Jean. "A measly five thousand dollars?"

The judge doesn't respond. He gets up and slips out a door behind his bench and that's the last we see of him.

Penny Jean goes up to Henry Junior and pleads with him, saying five thousand dollars is a joke when you take into consideration the years she spent in therapy and separated from her mother and all.

Henry Junior agrees. Ollie and I are sitting in the front with Susie Nesbitt so we hear what Henry says. He tells her they can go back and appeal the sentence, but the chances are slim that they'll get a different judge because McWorter is the circuit judge assigned to Berrington County, and he's a stubborn man, not likely to change his mind.

Penny Jean stamps her foot and says another trial is out of the question. She says she's going to sell the Hillcrest property and get the hell back to California. Sandy Sanderson, who comes up and stands by her side, explains that Penny Jean can't stomach another trial, plus he himself can't be taking off any more time from his job in an ice-cream store in Fresno.

I stand up to look over and see how George Bauer is taking it, but he's nowhere to be seen. He must have been led out already. Then, who's suddenly standing in front of me but Old Lady Heffington, trying to sweet-talk me into coming and staying in her house. She says my room is still open and it won't cost me a penny and she's put in a supply of new linens, and on and on like that. I try to shake her off, but she won't shake. The poor woman follows me out into the hallway and outside and down the front steps of the courthouse, talking about sheets and towels and such.

I level with her. "Look, Mrs. Heffington, I need my sunshine, I need my palm trees, I need my Atlantic Ocean. We only came home to testify, and we're heading back to Florida as soon as Ollie gets the car gassed up."

Which, even though I thought it was true, turns out to be false.

Because when Ollie comes out, I ask him, "When we leavin'?" and he says—right there in front of Mrs. Heffington—that he's not going back to Florida. He gives me a spiel about how he doesn't fit the Florida style of faith, says it pains him to have to disappoint me, but he's going back to preaching around the old hometown.

"Style of faith!" I tell him. "What do you mean 'style of faith'? Ain't but one style of faith as far as I know, either you believe or you don't believe."

He admits then that he misspoke. He says, "You're right, Grover, I should have said 'style of worship.' I simply don't fit the style of worship down South."

Which is only part of his reason if you ask me because all the while he's talking to me he's making eyes at Susie Nesbitt. So I figure he wants to stay home and court Susie. I'd say he's letting himself in for a whole pack of trouble, but it's his funeral, not mine.

And now that I'm in Coral Gables for the second time, I've been watching the church programs on TV, and I think I know what bothers Ollie about the way people worship down here. It's the way they interrupt the preacher all the time, saying "Ah-huh," "Amen," and "You tell 'em, Brother." In all the churches in Staggerford—and I been to every one of them, for funerals mostly—they hold their tongues till it's hymn time. Ollie never likes to be interrupted.

Anyhow, Mrs. Heffington's still hanging on me when Ollie says he's not going back, and her eyes light up and she says, "Oh, Grover, now you'll need a place to live," but I put an end to that in a hurry. I tell her I got a place for tonight at the Thrifty Springs Motel, and tomorrow I'm starting out for the South, even if I have to hitchhike.

Which is what I do, because I don't have money enough for the bus. I hitch a ride right away with a trucker traveling all the way to Sauk Rapids, who sings songs all the way, country western numbers I've never cared much for, but they seem to make him happy. I'm standing in Sauk Rapids no more than two minutes when a guy who's going into the Twin Cities picks me up in a big, old Lincoln. Heck, this hitchhiking is a breeze—I beat the bus to Minneapolis by a good hour.

That's what I think the first day. By the middle of the second day, standing in a dinky town somewhere north of Lafayette, Indiana, and freezing my hands and feet off, I'm plenty sick of hitchhiking. The sky clouds over and a cold rain starts to fall. I don't see the sun and warm up until I get down south of Atlanta, my fourth day out.

I catch a ride across the state line into Florida with a guy in a brand-new minivan packed full of his belongings, who obviously picks me up because he needs somebody to tell his troubles to. His name is Herman Schroeder. He says his troubles all started when he was a little kid during World War II, and his daddy was in the navy, stationed in San Diego. He says his momma got a call right after Christmas from an officer who said his daddy'd been shot in San Diego harbor, and she should come right away and see him in the hospital. It sounded urgent, like he was going to die.

"How did he get shot?" I ask the man.

"I'll get to that," he says. He goes on to tell me how poor his family was. His daddy never sent money home from the navy. They lived in Ohio and didn't have enough money for his momma to travel clear across the country, so she went to her brothers and they all pitched in and she bought herself a bus ticket and took Herman along. Herman was just a little shaver, five or six, at the time. "You ever spent four days and four nights on a Greyhound bus?" he asks me, and I tell him no, I never did. "Well, for a little kid it's hell, especially when your momma's crying her eyes out all the way, saying 'What will we do without your poor daddy?' That's when I figured out there's something more between a husband and wife than meets the eye, because I was getting along just fine without him and I couldn't figure out why she missed him so much."

"He was a mean bastard, huh?" I put in.

"Oh, my daddy wasn't mean so much as he was a man with too many friends," he says. "My daddy was always thinking of other people and never paid any attention to his family. One day he drove me downtown and went into a bar and left me in the car for four hours. He came out half lit, and drove home as though nothing was wrong. Another time he was baby-sitting when my momma had to go to the doctor and the older kids started a fire in their bedroom. I had two older brothers and an older sister. My daddy was on the telephone talking to one of his buddies and never called the fire department until every room was full of smoke and the house was burned so bad we had to find another place to live.

"Well, sir, we get to San Diego and it's already dark when we find our way to the hospital," he says. "We expect Daddy to be hovering near death, but we find him whooping it up with some other people in the lobby. It's New Year's Eve and they're having themselves a high old time—balloons and funny hats and all. He sees me and momma and hollers at us to come join the fun, as if he'd just seen us five minutes ago. Momma goes up to him and says, 'Lester, we thought you was dyin',' and he says, 'Naw, I got shot, but only a little,' and he opens his bathrobe and pulls up his pajama shirt and shows us the wound off to the side of his belly button. When Momma sees how small the scab is and how nice it's healing she gets mad and happy at the same time. 'Oh, Lester,' she says, and she beats her fists on his chest and tells him there was an officer called her up and said he was terribly wounded, and he says 'Oh, that was just Ensign So-and-so, he's an alarmist,' and Momma ends up laughing in his arms. They start dancing to some music on the radio, and I go to sleep on a nice, padded bench over the heat register."

This story of Herman's doesn't have what you'd call a tragic ending, so I ask him what all this has to do with the troubles in his life and he says, "I'll tell you later. Where you headed?" I tell him Coral Gables, and he takes the fork in the freeway leading down the Atlantic coast. I don't think any-thing of it until it gets to be late afternoon, after he's told me at least a dozen more stories, and we get to Coral Gables and he says, "Okay, now where?" and I realize he's taking me to my door.

Then comes the big surprise. I'm getting out in front of my sister's condo and Herman Schroeder says, "How many units in this here building of yours?"

"Forty-two," I tell him, "each with an ocean view."

"Any for rent?"

"Not that I know of," I tell him, "but there's usually one or two for sale. Old retired people keep dying off."

He squints up at the building and says, "I planned on renting, but I'll buy if I have to."

"You live around here?" I ask him.

"I live in Grand Rapids, Michigan, but I'm moving down."

It isn't until he's settled in two floors below us and has come in for coffee and cookies every afternoon that I realize what he's up to. He drove me clear down from Atlanta because he needed a friend. Some days he just sits and looks out at the ocean the way I like to do. Other days he tells me about his life as a car dealer and about his kids who are scattered all over the United States, and about his wife who died a year ago come July the first.

It doesn't occur to me that I've got myself another Dusty on my hands until the day I'm going through the latest issue of the *Weekly* and Herman Schroeder says, "Grover, do you know you squint when you read? You ought to see an eye doctor."

It's sort of interesting what he says about his wife's last days though. She was pretty well out of it, lying in the hospital dying, when all of a sudden one night she opened her eyes and said the pope wanted her to enter a convent. The nurse told her never mind, but she got real agitated, and when Herman came to the hospital in the morning she was still going on about it because the pope told her in no uncertain terms to go and be a nun. Then to everybody's relief she went into a coma, but every once in a while she'd come out of it and start up all over again about the pope telling her what to do. According to Herman she had always been a little nutty on the subject of religion, but this was the first time she ever talked about becoming a nun. Finally, after another day of this delusion, her sister and Herman were visiting the hospital and they hatched this idea of writing a letter from the pope excusing her from entering the convent. They got a sheet of paper from the nurse's station and they wrote it out in the family room down the hall, and they went in and Herman read it to her, and it worked like magic. She relaxed and spent another day or so in a coma and died peacefully.

"What did she die of?" I ask him.

"I'll get back to that," he tells me, and he starts in on another story about a man he knew who stole things from gas stations.

It isn't a bad life. I expect to spend the rest of my earthly days listening to Herman Schroeder. I'm learning to tune him out when I want to and listen when it's interesting. I still miss Dusty and Ollie, but I'll get over it. I'll never go back to Staggerford before Mrs. Heffington dies. I'll never go back till they build another hotel like the Ransford. I'll never go back till it stops being cold there in the wintertime.

THE
Life and Death of
Nancy Clancy's
Nephew

1

❖

WHEN W. D. NESTOR WAS asked at the age of seventy-two why he was unable to express any emotion but anger, he thought for half a minute, then said he supposed it was for lack of a role model.

It was Dr. H. Herbert Henderson who asked the question. W.D. had been driven to Rookery and dropped off by his daughter, Viola, and it wasn't until he saw the doctor's title on the office door that he realized he was about to undergo the third degree at the hands of a psychiatrist. Viola had simply said that he had a medical appointment.

"Do you mean as a boy?" asked Dr. Henderson, leaning back in his soft chair and lighting his pipe.

"Yeah, growing up on the farm."

"And you never saw people be sad or cry or give vent to their feelings?"

"Oh, yeah, my mother, but my dad never did, nor any of the men I knew in those days."

"Tell me about them, Mr. Nestor, your mother and father." This Henderson was the damnedest doctor W.D. had ever been to. Instead of a white smock, he wore a camel-hair sport coat and smoked a pipe, and his office was furnished like a living room.

"Well, my dad," said W.D., "he was just your average farmer back then. Tight-lipped. Hard worker. He used to get mad at the cows once in a while when he was milking, but that's about it."

"Did he ever get mad at you?"

W.D. took a while to think back, then he said, "Oh, sure, whenever I misbehaved."

"And how would he show his anger?"

"He'd get out the belt."

"And what belt was that, Mr. Nestor?"

Jesus, what a dumbbell this guy was, thought W.D. He'd probably never even been threatened, let alone whipped, by a belt in his life. "Any belt that was handy," he replied.

"So what do you mean, 'he got out the belt'?"

"It was what we said instead of 'whipping us.' That's what getting out the belt means."

"Oh, my goodness." Dr. Henderson took his pipe out of his mouth, laid a delicate hand on his chest, and coughed almost silently. "You were whipped as a boy?"

"Sure."

"And you mean he whipped others in your family? You said 'whipping *us*.'"

W.D. nodded. "My brother, other guys I knew at school. Farm boys mostly."

"More than one of the other boys, would you say?"

"All of 'em."

"All of them were whipped? Dear, dear." The doctor

shook his head sadly as he wrote something on a pad of paper. Then he gave W.D. a pitying look and said, "And your mother?"

"Let's see, my mother, she was pretty typical, I guess, although I didn't know many other women real well, so I can't say for sure. She did the inside work—you know, cooking and washing clothes and all that."

"And did she get angry, too?"

"No. Leastwise not very often. She used to blow her stack when the fire went out in the kitchen range and the woodbox'd be empty and she'd have to go out and chop some more wood. But that was only when me and my brother were too little to go out and do it. When we got old enough she'd send us out to chop wood."

"Did she whip you, too?"

Boy, where did this guy come from? He didn't understand a damn thing about life on the farm. W.D. was losing patience with him. He said, "No, mothers never did that. She'd tell Dad and he'd get out the belt when he came in from the barn."

The doctor jotted something more down on his notepad. Then he said, "So anger was all you saw from your mother as well as your father."

"Oh, no, that's not true. My mother had moods. She'd be laughing one day and crying the next."

"But you said you had no role model for expressing emotion."

"That's right. Every man I knew kept himself pretty well bottled up."

"But your mother . . ."

W.D. got to his feet and slipped into his denim jacket. "Lesson's over, Doctor."

"What do you mean?"

"I mean I taught you enough about farm life for one day."

"But we have forty minutes left." He looked crestfallen as W.D. crossed his office to the door.

Before going out, W.D. turned and said, "No self-respecting farmboy of my generation would copy his mother."

❖

WHEN VIOLA PICKED him up in the Buick, W. D. Nestor told her she'd played him a dirty trick, bringing him to a psychiatrist under false pretenses. He'd thought it was time for his blood-pressure and cholesterol checkup.

Viola, who had put on her new jeans and her best flowered shirt for this trip to Rookery, said, "Pops, I spent the last hour with Aunt Nancy."

"Nancy Clancy?"

She nodded. "She's got to be over ninety. She's got dewlaps like a turkey."

The mention of his old aunt made W.D. thoughtful. "I suppose I ought to go see her myself before she dies." He remembered times when his wife was living and Nancy Clancy would show up for holiday dinners, at which she was not loved but admired like an heirloom and always delivered home earlier than she wished.

"When she kicks the bucket, somebody's going to get a bunch of mighty nice antiques from that old dame." Viola snapped her gum. "What did the doctor tell you?"

"Didn't tell me nothing. Just asked me a bunch of stupid questions."

Viola nodded. "That's the way they work." Since marrying Kermit Kilbride several years ago, Viola seemed like a changed person. Her father remembered her as a slight little thing in dresses; now she was fat and wore nothing but jeans. She and Kermit had no children. W.D. wondered why *his* two children had grown up to be such difficult people. His wife, Lucille, had been easygoing, and he himself had not made impossible demands on them—unless, in his son's case, you considered getting out of bed at ten o'clock in the morning impossible. His lazy son, called Sonny, would have spent his whole life in bed if W.D. had let him. Sonny couldn't stand farm work. He left home at eighteen and neither W.D. nor Lucille ever heard from him again.

"But he must have said something," said Viola.

"Who?"

"The doctor."

"Ach, that doc doesn't know a damn thing about farm life. I had to tell him what stuff meant, like somebody getting out the belt."

"So what did he say about your problem?"

"What problem? I don't have a problem."

"You getting mad at Kermit all the time."

"Listen, Viola, Kermit is so bullheaded the only way to handle him is to get mad at him. You know that. I've heard you do it yourself. He gets on a subject and he can't let it go. All last winter he kept talking about starting up a corn-and-hog operation till I thought I'd go nuts."

"You can't blame him for that. It's what he came from, corn and hogs."

"Well, he isn't where he came from anymore. He's been working with my turkeys now for . . . how many years? When did you and Kermit get married?"

"Seventeen years, come October. And they aren't your turkeys, Pops. It was Kermit signed the contract when they came in in May, and he signed the note at the bank for the summer's supply of turkey mash. So it's Kermit's neck on the line, not yours."

W.D. quit arguing. Viola always took Kermit's side. He looked at the buildings they passed on the outskirts of Rookery, and when they got out in the country he studied the farmland. All of it looked about as sandy and dried up as his own 120 acres near Bartlett, not good for much except raising turkeys or sheep. Viola spoke occasionally, but W.D. paid no attention, for he was thinking about Dr. Henderson and remembering his boyhood on the farm. His wife, Lucille, used to call him stoical, and he guessed he was. He recalled the first time he was conscious of reining in his feelings. It was the day his brother was killed and the feeling was grief.

His brother, Albert, was a year older than W.D. He was accidentally shot by a hunter who evidently mistook one of the Nestors' cows for a deer and missed the cow. The hunter was never found. Instant death, the coroner said later, the shot catching Albert smack in the forehead and dropping him like a sack of feed. He'd just turned twenty-one the week before. It happened next to the pasture gate behind the barn. He lay there through most of the afternoon before he was found by W.D., who came in from hunting in the woods along the creek bottom below the farm. There was still an hour of daylight, but W.D. gave up early because he'd seen no deer all day and he felt as though his feet were freezing. Now, over fifty years later, he could still remember the electric heat of shock that coursed through his body when he saw his brother lying dead. One of the calves was sniffing the blood. He ran to the house and into the kitchen, where his mother was cooking supper in her new electric oven. Standing there with his four-ten shotgun in his hands, he said no thank you to a piece of pie before he told her what he had seen crumpled on the ground next to the pasture gate. Half a minute passed before she understood, and then she ran outside, but before she rounded the corner of the barn she knew she dared not look and she ran back to the kitchen, breathlessly repeating, "Holy God, don't shoot me, Warren," and she cranked the phone on the wall and said three times into the mouthpiece, "Help! Warren's killing us, help!" and then she ran outside and hid in the henhouse.

Those on the telephone party line were the first to arrive. Ernestine Weber drove the Webers' old black Plymouth with cream cans standing where the backseat used to be, and Mrs. O'Brien ran the quarter mile from her place with her apron on. "Warren's got a gun, he shot Albert!" his mother screamed through a broken window of the henhouse.

Well, of course W.D. had done no such thing. The coroner, Dr. Phillips, proved this when he showed up. Stepping carefully around the cowflops in the pasture and turning W.D.'s four-ten over in his hands, he said, "This boy was shot by a deer rifle, not this toy," and he handed the four-ten back to W.D. There were six or eight people at the farm by this time, a car and a pickup having followed Dr. Phillips and his wife out from town. Even after the undertaker came for the body, the men were reluctant to join the women in the kitchen. This being opening day of deer season, the men spoke of hunting as they walked in small circles, bent forward at the waist, their hands in their pockets and shivering, for now, at dusk, a cold rain like pins was beginning to slant across the prairie.

"Did you hear what happened to Jake Altoff today?"

"No."

"Jake shot a doe over by Loomis this noon and the same bullet killed a fawn he didn't see that was standing right next to her, so he called the game warden, told him what he done, killed two, one by accident, and the game warden said, 'Just stay right there, I'll be out and take care of it,' and Jake waited for an hour and gutted out the two deer and every-thing—and the game warden come out and fined him a hun-dred dollars and took both deer."

"Jesus."

"I'll be damned."

"If I was him . . ."

"Who was the game warden?"

"Well, what would you expect? If he didn't fine Jake everybody'd be shooting two deer by accident."

"But he turned himself in."

"Jake's a damn fool."

The rain grew heavier as W.D.'s father, who had been hunting farther north with friends, drove into the yard. "What's going on?" he asked, seeing the crowd of men. When he was told, he lowered his head and cursed, then went behind the barn for a look at the spot where it happened. The men followed. He cursed again and asked W.D., "How's your mother taking it?"

"Not real good."

"We better go in, then," said his father, and he led the group single file into the kitchen. They found his mother sitting silently on a chair while the three women chattered about what they would serve in the church basement after the funeral. His mother was obviously having trouble getting her breath. Each time she inhaled, her diaphragm jumped and immediately expelled the air. Hyperventilation, Dr. Phillips called it as he ushered her into the small living room where the flame in the oil burner cast an orange light out through its isinglass aperture. He told her to lie on the couch, but on her back she choked, so he propped her up in a sitting position with pillows. Meanwhile, W.D. and the other men in the kitchen heard Ernestine Weber saying that she'd bring a fruit salad to the funeral. Mrs. O'Brien said she would bake two apple pies. "What a good year for apples," she added.

"Oh, I know it," exclaimed Mrs. Phillips, the coroner's wife, pouring out cups of coffee. "You should see the Rome Beauties the Fairway Store in Bartlett got in yesterday."

Despite being nineteen years old, W.D., sitting at the kitchen table, was about to shed a few tears—it was permitted; he'd seen a neighbor boy, a teenager, crying at the funeral of his father a year or so earlier—when his mother suddenly appeared in the doorway to the living room, still dry-eyed and looking deranged, asking, "Where's my Albert? Where did he go?"

This frightened the urge to cry out of W.D. Using his father's example, and despite his grief over losing his brother as well as his sorrow over his mother's thinking he had been capable of shooting him, he shed no tears that day or at any time afterward—not until the final weeks of his life, over sixty years later.

2

❖

AT SUNRISE W.D. walked from the house out to the turkey lot, hung his cap on a fence post, and began to run. Heavy, white turkeys, wide-eyed and ungainly, clucked and fluttered out of his way and the whole flock, nearly seven thousand birds, began to surge from one feeding station to another, hungry for breakfast. The turkey lot was more than a lot, it was a forty-acre field, a quarter mile on each side, and W.D.'s track was the perimeter of the field, a path inside the fence line worn hard by years of running. Spring, summer, and fall, W.D. ran a mile a day. Years ago his running had been something to see. His lungs were good then and he ran the four sides of the turkey lot like a stallion, with his head held high and his pace steady and effortless, but now in his seventies, his style was gone and with the planting of each foot, he shot an elbow or a wrist out from his side. In his loose blue shirt and overalls he went flailing along the fence line like a turkey trying to fly.

He ran the first quarter mile and stopped to rest, panting, his hands on his knees. This was the corner of the lot where a small pen held the sick turkeys. W.D. made a clucking noise in his throat and put his hand through the wire, snapping his fingers, but only one of the birds turned its head. What creature under the sun looks as hopeless as a sick turkey? You see the sick one in the flock, hanging back at mealtime, holding its head to one side and staring at the sun, or leaning against a post and silently opening and closing its beak. It must be suffering from worms or pip, or something worse like pneumonia or despair, and if you do not rush it to the sick pen when the symptoms first appear it will be set upon and pecked to death by the healthy turkeys. One of the turkeys in the pen, a bird with sores on its head, staggered over to peck at W.D.'s finger. Then it lost heart at the last minute and hung its head, resting the point of its beak on a pebble. W.D. counted twenty birds in the pen, twice as many as usual.

He set off along the south side of the lot, running into the low sun. W.D.'s running dated back several years, to the days when he used to visit the public library and check out videos. This was when his wife was still alive and the two of them spent whole evenings sitting in front of their old Zenith TV set, watching classic miniseries like *Roots* and *Brideshead Revisited* or *National Geographic* specials or collections of old newsreels. He kept a picture of Lucille taped to the wall in his bedroom. It was clipped from the monthly newsletter of the Holy Family Rest Home in Bartlett. It showed Lucille sitting up in bed and staring emptily straight ahead—her typical Alzheimer's look—her hair pulled back in her grandmotherly bun, her hands lying limply on a braided rug, which covered her almost to the armpits and ran down toward the camera in slopes and folds like a blossoming meadow. Beside her stood the Reverend Bob Buckingham, grinning at the photographer and pinching the edge of the rug. It was his rug. The caption said that because it was the fiftieth rug Lucille had braided in six months' time, the reverend had given her twenty dollars for it and promised to buy her hundredth as well. In the accompanying article, which W.D. didn't save, the reader was told that it was Reverend Buckingham's encouragement that started Lucille Nestor on this rigorous project, and the entire town of Bartlett was delivering their rags to the rest home for Lucille to make rugs out of. She looked, in the photo, like a woman who'd braided her last rug. Her head hung forward, it seemed, in exhaustion. W.D., seeing this, drove straight to the Home and forbade her to continue, forbade the staff to allow her any more rags. He knew how conscientious she was, even in her right mind, and he could see that because a clergyman had told her to produce those rugs—they were heavy as sod—she was obviously working at it day and night and wearing herself out. Using a secret stash of rags and old neckties she kept in her closet, she started another rug despite his prohibition, but she died before it was finished.

It was a newsreel they watched together that started W.D. running, an item about the Olympic runner from Finland, Paavo Nurmi. The Finn seemed to float across the grainy screen of the old news clip, and W.D. was reminded of the joy of running in his boyhood: running from his house to the neighbor's where he used to hire out at harvest time, running left and right down the frozen, bending river, a shortcut to the country school he went to; running out from the barn to bring in the cows for milking, picking up speed down the pasture slopes until the chilly air of evening was a wind in his face. Running always made him feel good, and feeling good made him want to run. Sometimes in his dreams, since Lucille died, life was a mile and he could not run.

A pair of toms ran with him for a rod or so, then dropped away. "What's the matter? Can't you keep up?" He was speaking, not to the turkeys, but to the reporters he imagined them to be. It was a fantasy he had invented in 1945, when newspapers carried pictures of Harry Truman in his morning walks down Pennsylvania Avenue. To W.D. the President looked like a man who knew the joy of a good run; it was probably his concern for the winded reporters who were scribbling in their little notepads that kept the President from breaking into a sprint. *Mr. Nestor, are you making optimum use of your land?* the reporters seemed to be asking this morning (*optimum* was the big word this year in the farming journals), *and shouldn't you be raising more turkeys?* "Not by a damn sight," blurted W.D. His voice was jolted as he ran. "A healthy turkey is an uncrowded turkey." *Mr. Nestor, the voters are wondering, instead of hauling water to the feeding stations in a truck, why haven't you piped water to the feeding stations?* "In the first place it would take almost a mile of pipe, and in the second place in the winter the pipes would freeze up and bust. Tell the voters to use the brains God gave them." *Mr. Nestor, is there truth to the rumor that these turkeys do not really belong to you?* "All right, so they belong to the Basil Underwood

Packing Company. It's the way turkey growing is handled these days. It's only a technicality."

It was true. Nowadays the farmer signed a contract with the processor. The processor paid for the chicks, and when pickup day arrived in the fall, he hauled them off by the truckload to his plant. The farmer was merely a caretaker, bringing the birds through the summer as carefully as possible, so that he could collect all the contract called for. W.D. didn't like to raise birds under contract, because it left him no pride of ownership and no opportunity to play the turkey market; in a word it left him no risk—but it was taken out of W.D.'s hands long ago. It was his son-in-law, Kermit, who signed the contracts and fed the turkeys now. "It isn't like it was," W.D. said to the reporters as he came to the southeast corner of the lot, and having run a half a mile, he sat on the ground with his back against a fence post. The thistle and goldenrod in the adjoining fields were silver with dew and the ripening corn in the neighbor's field beyond was the color of brass. Looking back at the cluster of buildings that had been his lifelong home—the house, the empty corn crib, the new machine shed, the old barn—he saw a pickup drive into the yard and he saw his son-in-law, Kermit, emerge from the back door of the house. It was one of the green and red pickups belonging to the Basil Underwood Packing Company that showed up every two weeks or so. Kermit stood beside it, talking. W.D. couldn't be sure because of the great distance, but he imagined the driver scanning the turkey lot and focusing his attention on the sick pen. The man from the packing company would naturally be fretting about the twenty sick turkeys and reminding Kermit, in an accusing tone that would make you want to run him off your place—or at least turn your back on him—that the birds must be fed and watered by the clock and the manure under the roosts must be carried away every day. It was like telling Viola how to cook and keep house, things she had been doing since she was a youngster. In Kermit's place, rather than stand there and be preached at, W.D. would have walked away and left the Underwood man with no choice but to turn around and drive away.

Kermit, for all his bluster, wasn't hard-boiled enough to be a good farmer. He'd start out strong, telling the field man that he knew twice as much about growing turkeys than anybody else in the county, but he always folded fast. The field man would remind him that every sick turkey was a loss of anywhere from three to four dollars cold cash, depending on the market, and Kermit would say he knew that as well as the next man and he was doing his best and he couldn't do any better than that. The field man would then say that's all he expected Kermit to do, his best, and he hoped there were no hard feelings. Kermit would say who said anything about hard feelings? And they would shake hands and go to the house for a cup of coffee. And sure enough, as W.D. watched, Viola appeared at the back step and called to the two men, and they walked across the yard together and entered the house.

The reporters seemed to be asking, *How would you handle the field man?* "I'd just let him talk himself out," W.D. said aloud. "I wouldn't flare up like Kermit does. What's the use? The packing company owns the birds and they own half the equipment on this farm and it's their paycheck that gets the three of us through the winter. When a farmer gets that beholden to somebody, the smartest thing he can do is keep his mouth shut." W.D. looked beyond the farm buildings to the blue hills on the horizon, the Thorn Hills where he used to hunt deer and squirrel. He rested his head back against the fence post and said, "I never knew a Nestor to bluster the way Kermit does. And the sad thing is that Viola has taken on his ways."

W.D. was awakened by the sound of the tank truck. The green and red pickup was gone from the yard and Kermit was driving into the turkey lot with the old International on which W.D. had installed a five-hundred-gallon water tank when he switched from a dairy to a turkey operation many years ago. The truck and the tank were covered with rust and the engine clacked like a tractor and backfired. Behind the truck, Kermit was pulling the new feed wagon, a high red wagon with rubber tires and a round green emblem on the side that said *Basil Underwood. Meat for the Millions.* W.D. rose and shook his right leg to loosen the crick in his hip and ran the third leg of his mile.

He didn't pause long at the northeast corner. Here the turkey manure was dumped and it was especially smelly now that it was being dug into every day. The township board, attempting to beautify a cemetery on a sandy hilltop, had bought rights to the pile and was sending a dump truck every day for a load of manure. It was carried away to the cemetery where it was spread in a four-inch layer over the graves of the township pioneers.

W.D.'s last quarter mile ran parallel with the highway. His stride had now become, with fatigue, a kind of skip, and it seemed to those passing in cars that he was making more movement up and down than forward. Accustomed to seeing him on their way to work, a few drivers honked, and W.D. gave them a wave or merely a nod, whichever gesture fit his mood of the moment.

Some old men wind up looking like their wives, Viola was fond of saying, but W.D. had overheard her tell a woman-friend one time that he had wound up looking like the turkeys on his farm. He thought she was probably right. His eyes were green and haughty and without lashes, and he carried himself with a strut that led the field men from the packing company to joke about the resemblance. Tom, they sometimes called him when they thought he was out of earshot. Well, W.D. thought his overweight son-in-law, Kermit, who came from a hog-and-corn operation, looked like a pig, with his fat red face, small eyes, and jowls that jiggled when he spoke.

W.D. picked his hat off the post and looked at his pocket watch—a forty-minute mile. He wiped his feet at the kitchen door and sat down at the table.

"Wipe your feet," said Viola.

"I did."

She stooped and looked at his shoes under the table, then served him his stewed prunes and two pancakes. "There's droppings in your cuffs," she said.

He ignored her, as he usually did at meals. "What happened to these?" he said, looking into his prune dish.

"They're pitted," said Viola.

W.D. put one in his mouth. "Why?"

"Why! What kind of question is that? You can't eat the pits, can you?"

"I never ate the pits when they weren't pitted."

Viola sat down at the table to paint her fingernails and the smell seared W.D.'s nostrils. "We had company," she said.

"I saw the truck."

"It was Basil Underwood himself."

"Basil Underwood?" W.D. hadn't seen Basil Underwood since the day they signed this year's contract in the spring. "If Basil Underwood is out making the rounds, who's back at the plant packing the meat?"

"He says you have to quit running in the turkey lot."

W.D. stopped chewing his prune.

"He says our losses are higher than any other farm this summer—fifteen, twenty birds a week. No sign of disease. No thunderstorms. Fifteen a week average for no reason at all. He says it must be your running."

Viola held her fingernails at a distance.

W.D. pushed his chair back. "Just what the hell connection does Basil Underwood see between sick turkeys and me running?"

"Running makes the birds nervous."

W.D. blinked his lashless eyes. "Do you believe that?"

Viola shrugged and took up her brush again.

"Turkeys are too dumb to get nervous."

His daughter chuckled, then added, "He says he'd never put horses in with steers. Horses get frisky and run and then the steers get frisky and run instead of standing there getting fat."

"There aren't enough brains in Basil Underwood's head to wad a shotgun." He rose and walked out the door.

"Finish your prunes," Viola called through the screen.

"I never heard such poppycock. I make the turkeys nervous? It's the turkeys make *me* nervous, if the truth was known."

"You haven't finished your prunes."

"Throw 'em out. They took out the flavor with the pits."

❖

WHEN KERMIT FINISHED feeding and watering the turkeys he said the same thing. Basil Underwood was dead set against anybody running amongst his birds.

"And what did you tell him?" asked W.D. He was sitting on the bench under the burr oak in the side yard.

"I didn't tell him nothing. Except it would fry your ass."

"And then what did he say?"

Kermit's big stomach jumped with laughter. He was holding a cup of hot coffee and spilling it down the front of his blue overalls.

"Come on. What did he say then?" W.D. hated the way fat men laughed.

"He said your ass has been fried before." Kermit shook until he burned his hand and dropped the cup on the grass.

"And what was so funny about that?"

"Just the way it struck me."

"Listen here now, Kermit. Do you swallow everything they stuff down your throat, him and his field men? I always thought they were narrow between the ears and this proves it. You don't expect me to quit running my mile, do you? I've been running the mile there for eighteen, twenty years."

"You've just run your last mile in that turkey lot, W.D. Father-in-law or not, I told him you wouldn't run in there again until the birds was gone in November. I know on the home place we never let dogs in the pigpen."

"This isn't your home place, Kermit. This is my place and I've been running around that turkey lot since nineteen eighty-three."

"W.D., do you know what those birds will likely bring this year?"

"I don't care what they bring."

"Just guess once."

"Okay, a good year. Everybody says so. Three-sixty apiece."

"Guess again. Higher."

"Three-sixty-five."

"Basil Underwood says four-forty. Four dollars and forty cents a head. Now for that kind of money you can stop running." Kermit picked up his cup and went into the kitchen for a refill.

W.D. sat studying a hilly field of ripening corn across the highway.

❧

THE NEXT DAY, using the odometer on the old International, W.D. measured a half mile on the road running beside the hilly cornfield across the highway; then he set off running. The road was too steep. By the time he reached the top of the first hill he felt as if he had already run his mile, but he had yet to run up to the crest of the next hill and then turn around and run all the way back to the highway. It began to rain. Between the two hills he let himself down the steep bank of a creek and sat under the bridge to keep dry. The red-sand bottom gave a purple glow to the water, and although it was roiling, he caught glimpses of tiny trout darting upstream and down. W.D. fastened his eyes on a small eddy gurgling under the exposed root of a willow.

How old is that little whirlpool? he was asked by reporters, and he considered the years that water had been dipping and spinning there before going on to the waters of the Badbattle River and in turn its meeting with the Red River of the North and its trip around Winnipeg; its diversion through the dozens of lakes of Manitoba and Ontario and its coming together once more to pour itself into Hudson Bay; its final disbursement into the oceans of the world, into the clouds of the sky, into the rains of summer. It occurred to him that, like himself, the world was very old and set in its ways.

W.D. was roused by thunder, or was it a car passing overhead on the bridge? The rain was letting up. He brushed the sand off the seat of his pants, climbed the bank to the gravel road, and alternately running and walking he reached the crest of the second hill, from which, in the hazy mist, he could see neither the Thorn Hills to the west nor the town of Bartlett to the east, both scarcely four miles away. He walked gingerly now; the soles of his tennis shoes had been worn thin and the edges of the gravel, exposed by the rain, stood up from the road and hurt his feet. When he reached the bottom of the hill the rain fell faster. He sat under the bridge until noon, when Kermit came looking for him.

3

❖

IN MID-AFTERNOON the rain passed and the sun came out
and steamed the fields. W.D., in dry clothes but still shivering, was set out on the back step like a young tomato plant
to soak up heat. "And don't let us catch you out on that road
again," Viola called through the screen door.

"Don't worry," said W.D. "That place is no good for running." He got up from the step and walked around to the
bench and sat under the burr oak, remembering a happier
time, before Viola had thrown in her lot with Kermit, before
Lucille had died. He recalled, with pleasure, his wedding day
nearly fifty years ago.

W.D. and Lucille had eloped. It was a day of high but re-
pressed emotion for W.D. and the emotions he restrained
were anxiety, joy, and frustration. Lucille, an orphan, had
been brought up on a farm in the soil-rich Badbattle River
valley by an aunt, a very strict maiden lady named Velma
Schuler. Aunt Velma had no cattle and raised no crops. She
supported herself and her niece by renting out her land to
neighboring farmers.

It was in the spring of 1952, a late spring of snowdrifts and muddy roads, that he and Lucille had eloped. In the ditches beside the road that W.D. drove that morning the snow was deep, but in the fields patches of moist black earth were enlarging after two or three days of warm sun. He sailed past the driveway with the mailbox bearing the name Schuler, and he did not stop until he reached the dip in the road where Lucille said she'd be waiting, out of sight of her aunt in the farmhouse. And there she was, holding an armload of her schoolbooks and dressed in her best Sunday coat and dress. He reached across and opened the passenger door. She got in quickly, they said "Hi," and they sped away.

Climbing out of the river valley, Lucille's head on his shoulder, he drove into thin veils of snow and saw that the weather was changing. Crossing the prairie, he saw no horizon, for the snow here was falling generally and evenly, and farmsteads and fencerows and distant trees had a very soft look about them. He drove west under a cloud as deep blue as a late evening summer sky, and he remembered the heavy indigo sky that rolled over the farm once or twice each winter or spring and left drifts of snow on the roads as high as a truck.

"What's the matter, Warren?" said Lucille, for he seemed anxious.

"Nothing, why?"

"Are we going to be on time?"

"Plenty of time. We can stop for coffee in Rookery." He accelerated to sixty-five on the straight highway.

"Wonderful," she said. Rookery was as far as Lucille had ever traveled from home, and then only once. A month earlier, on March 8, the day after her eighteenth birthday, she and W.D. had sneaked away to the Rookery courthouse for their marriage license.

Forty miles later, nearing Rookery, W.D. pulled off the highway at a trucker's restaurant. Stepping inside was like coming in out of the night, for the lights were bright and the morning sky had grown darker than it had been at dawn. Most of the booths and stools were occupied by truck drivers, all of whom, it seemed, were acquainted. They spoke and laughed loudly over their breakfast as though it were at a family meal. The tile floor was covered by black boot marks and little pools of melting snow.

They found an empty booth at the back, next to the kitchen door, and they held hands across the table. W.D.'s heart swelled with joy as he looked at Lucille. He loved her dimples, her dark eyes, and her lips. Her dimples deepened as she smiled and said, "I'm sure I won't be able to eat anything."

"Nervous?" he asked.

"I'm fine until I start to eat. Aunt Velma made oatmeal this morning, but I couldn't eat it."

"Ma made me oatmeal, too," he said. He didn't admit that he couldn't finish his either.

His mother had thought this curious because ordinarily he licked up a second bowl. His mother asked if he was sick. "No," he said, "only I'm getting married today." This was news to his mother. "You're joking," she said, though she never knew him to joke. "Nope," he said. "Is it Lucille?" she asked. "Yep," he said, concluding as lengthy a conversation as he and his mother had had since the death of his father last fall. With his father and brother dead, W.D., at the age of twenty-three, was in charge of the farm and all its equipment, including the Oldsmobile because his mother didn't drive.

After breakfast, he went up to his bedroom and came down wearing his suit and a necktie. "It's a fine thing when your mother isn't invited to your wedding," she told him. He explained then that it was a secret because Lucille's aunt Velma was sure to raise holy hell when she found out. They would continue to live apart till Lucille graduated in May. His mother nodded. She knew Velma Schuler from church and what a temperamental and strict woman she was. "Where are you getting married?" she asked. "Abernathy," he said. "Abernathy? Where's that?" "It's way west of here. Joe Smiddick is a minister in Abernathy." Joe Smiddick had been a high school classmate of W.D.'s. As he crossed the kitchen to leave, his mother did an unusual thing. She grabbed him by the shoulders and planted a kiss on his cheek.

At the open end of the horseshoe counter a boy in a chef's hat stood at the stove, grilling eggs and pancakes and glancing up at the order slips hanging on a wire near his head. His hat had lost its starch and hung over his ear like a baggy tam. There were two waitresses, the smaller of whom must have been new on the job because during every spare moment she made coy conversation with the cook, teasing and blushing, while the other waitress, who appeared to be in her late twenties, worked like a veteran, supplying each trucker to his satisfaction with casual insults and hot coffee. She moved efficiently along the counter and over to their booth. Quickly sizing them up as lovers, she said, "Why do some people find their heart's desire right off the bat while others have to search a lifetime? I myself had two marriage proposals before I was twenty-five, one right here over the cash register during a lull in business, the other in a car parked out at the cemetery, and I turned them both down because I thought I could do better. But I never did. If I knew then what I know now I'd've accepted the proposal over the cash register. He was kind of a nerd in those days, but he went on to vocational school and got a good job as a tool and dye maker, whatever that is, and he's got a nice car and a wife and a house and a strong reputation among the mothers of girls who turned him down. So what'll you guys have?"

W.D. ordered two coffees and toast.

A skinny old man in a long coat entered the restaurant and held the door open for his wife, who moved in slowly with both hands clutching the door frame. She was old and very large and covered by a coat of red fur that didn't meet in front. Her gray hair, piled in a bun at the back of her head, was coming undone and the stiff spirals of hair waved like feathers in the breeze. While she caught her breath, her slight husband stood at her side, glancing about for a place to sit. Two stools at the counter were vacant, and he pointed to them, but she shook her head. However, because there was nowhere else, he pulled her gently over to a stool and eased her down on it. To accommodate her size, he and the man on the other side had to lean away from her.

"Warren, let's give them our booth," said Lucille.

"Yes, let's," said W.D.

Exchanging places, the old man smiled his thanks while his wife shuffled over to the booth, tipping from side to side as she moved, and spilled herself into the seat. The young waitress who had been sparring with the cook watched with her mouth open.

From the counter Lucille could see outside. "It's snowing harder," she said, piling her toast on top of W.D.'s.

He glanced outside. It looked like evening.

"What if we can't make it home tonight?" she asked, trying to sound calm.

"We'll make it. There's no wind." He spread jelly on his toast. "We'll start back as soon as the ceremony's over."

Back in the car, Lucille asked again if W.D. was certain they'd make it home by supper time.

"I'm positive," he said. "We've only got another fifty miles to go. We can be on our way back by noon."

Slowly and steadily the snow fell across the prairie and lay undisturbed through the dark, still morning, except along the highway where it was continually stirring in the wake of traffic. Oncoming trucks were followed by blinding clouds of snow, and W.D. slowed almost to a stop each time he saw one coming.

They reached Abernathy around eleven thirty. There wasn't much going on along Main Street. Two men stood visiting in the snow in front of the post office, a man came out of the liquor store, a woman was entering the grocer's. Main Street ended in a field of snow-covered farm equipment, and next to the field was the Abernathy Gospel Chapel, a small cement-block building with a flat roof and the words JESUS SAVES painted on the door in red letters.

W.D. helped Lucille out of the car and draped her coat around her shoulders. From the screened porch of a house across the street a man called to them and they hurried toward him, W.D. leading the way, leaving short-spaced prints in the deep snow for Lucille to follow. The porch was small and hanging beside the door was an old Christmas wreath that had turned the color of the rusted screen. Joe Smiddick, though W.D.'s age exactly, looked much more naive. He was no taller than Lucille, and with his light hair and eyelashes and his pink face she couldn't decide if he reminded her of a little boy or a very old man. He wore a wrinkled black suit. He slapped W.D. on the back and when he was introduced to Lucille he shook her hand warmly, saying, "I know you'll make a perfect wife for this lug." To W.D. he said quietly, as though in confidence, "Around here I'm known as the Little Preacher," then he gave out with a very loud laugh.

He led them into a tiny, neat living room where a large, elderly woman stood over the heat register in the floor. She wore a white wedding dress with a hoop skirt and a veil. "I want you to meet Mrs. Coker," said the Little Preacher, pulling the three of them together by their elbows. "Mrs. Coker lives next door and does my cooking and cleaning. She's a dear soul. Now you three get acquainted and have yourselves a lovely little talk while I call up Sammy Pitz and see what's keeping him. Sammy Pitz has agreed to be our other witness. You're a bit on the late side, aren't you? Aren't you later than you planned?"

"Probably," said W.D. "The snow."

"Not that it makes one iota of difference to me. It's your

wedding and you can take as much time as you wish. We're at your service, see, only Mrs. Coker put the chicken in at ten o'clock and it might be overdone by the time we're ready to eat. Can't you turn it down, Mrs. Coker?"

She replied in a deep voice. "I can turn it down." Then she asked Lucille to come with her.

As the Little Preacher spoke on the telephone in another room and Lucille followed Mrs. Coker up a narrow, dusty stairway, W.D. combed his hair, stooping to a small mirror over the piano.

"Sit down," said the minister, returning to the living room. "Sammy Pitz'll be delayed a few minutes. How are things on the farm? How are the roads? Have you met any of our classmates since I saw you last?"

W.D. sat on the piano bench and looked at his watch. "We were hoping to start back at twelve," he said. "Driving might be a problem."

"Nonsense, they keep the highways plowed. What do you think of Mrs. Coker showing up in her wedding dress? Is your bride at all sensitive to things like that? The old lady is really a dear soul. Her husband drinks and treats her miserably—a man of extremely poor judgment. But Mrs. Coker has found solace in the Word." Joe Smiddick began searching through a messy pile of papers on his small desk. "When I am called to a larger church, what will happen to Mrs. Coker and all the other poor souls who depend on me here in Abernathy? I've got my eye on a church in Rookery some day. Is your church thriving in Bartlett? How many people attend services on your typical winter Sunday? Ah, here it is." He waved a thick sheet of paper in the air. "We can't forget to sign this when it's over—the Certificate of Marriage." He found a pen in the drawer and bent over the desk, writing. "What's the bride's last name? I should know that, I remember her from school. Let's see, it's April 9 today."

"Schuler," said W.D. He spelled it for him.

"She's taller than I thought she'd be. And what county is she in?"

"Berrington, same as mine."

"I'll tell you how I first learned people were calling me the Little Preacher. I was over in Douglas one day—that's about twelve miles from here—and I introduced myself to the druggist and he said, 'Oh, so you're the Little Preacher. I understand you've brought the Abernathy church back from the dead.' Think of it, been here less than a year and already they know me in Douglas."

"Glad to hear it," said W.D.

"But I've had second thoughts about going the Gospel Tabernacle route. This is what I want to talk to you about, W.D. They say success lies with the Lutherans in these parts. Maybe if I'd've gone to a Lutheran seminary I'd be further along, know what I mean? I mean the Abernathy Gospel Tabernacle is pretty much the bush leagues."

W.D. went over and looked up the narrow stairwell. "Lutheran seminaries are for Lutherans," he said. "What's keeping them up there?"

"Don't worry, we can't start until Sammy gets here anyway."

Lucille appeared at the top of the stairs and came swiftly down. Mrs. Coker followed in a huff, saying, "Suit yourself, Sweetie. It's your funeral."

The Little Preacher responded as though to an alarm. He rushed to the stairs. "Now, now, Mrs. Coker, what's the trouble? Let's not start that again, Mrs. Coker."

W.D. took Lucille by the hand and led her to the sofa. It was a new sofa, cheap and hard as a bench. They sat and watched the Little Preacher nervously try to pacify Mrs. Coker, whose forehead had turned purple.

"There'll be no wedding march," she said. "Blondie here decided that for herself."

"Now, now, Mrs. Coker."

"I've been to more weddings than she has. I've been to more weddings than the three of you put together."

"Come and sit down, Mrs. Coker."

"Church or house, there's always a wedding march. And if there's a stairway, the bride marches down the stairs."

"Mrs. Coker."

"I'm going to turn down the chicken." She crossed the room with a rustle of petticoats, her veil trailing from her hairpins.

The Little Preacher sat down next to Lucille and took her hand. "You'll simply have to accept my apologies. She gets so worked up over weddings. You must try to see her side of it. Her own marriage is not a happy one, and every wedding to her is like a fresh start. She is to be pitied."

"She's nuts," said W.D.

Lucille smiled at the preacher, wiping her eyes. "I thought she wanted me to come down the stairs while she played the piano, but then I discovered that she wanted you to play and I was supposed to come down first like a bridesmaid, and she was to follow in her wedding dress."

"Honestly, I had no idea what she planned. I intended to

sing a song, but I expected her to play the piano." He turned to W.D, laughing. "If she had her way you might have married Mrs. Coker."

"God forbid."

"Let's get on with it," Mrs. Coker called from the kitchen. "We'll have to eat this bird inside half an hour."

There were footsteps on the porch and Joe Smiddick opened the door to Sammy Pitz, who went directly to the floor register and stood on it, panting, snow from his shoes dropping through the grating and sizzling on the furnace below. Sammy was a grocery clerk. He wore a green knee-length apron under his jacket. "Sorry I couldn't make it sooner," he said. "I was alone at the store till the boss got back from the bank." He looked younger than Lucille, and W.D. wondered what he was doing out of school. He nodded to W.D. and Lucille as the preacher introduced them, but their greetings were lost in the noise of banging pots from the kitchen.

"Okay, we're ready to roll," said the Little Preacher.

The wedding in the living room took four minutes. Mrs. Coker asked that she be excused because the chicken needed emergency treatment, and the preacher said she could be a witness from the kitchen.

He neither played nor sang, but standing shoulder to shoulder with the jacketed Sammy Pitz, he faced W.D. and Lucille and read solemnly from a little book. When he said "We are gathered here" the noise in the kitchen subsided and Mrs. Coker stood in the doorway watching. W.D. slipped a gold band on Lucille's finger and Lucille wept. Sammy Pitz said congratulations and shook the Little Preacher's hand and left. It was a minute before anyone else spoke. W.D. stood with his arm around Lucille's shoulders, and the preacher bowed his head. Mrs. Coker appeared to be in a trance.

"Well, let's eat," said the Little Preacher.

W.D. and Joe Smiddick ate chicken and peas and ice cream. Lucille, still unable to eat, sat with them at the kitchen table. Mrs. Coker, after the food was served, wrapped herself in a black shawl and stepped out the back door into the snow.

The Little Preacher wanted to know how W.D. was treated by Lutherans and Catholics. "Here in Abernathy it's possible to live out your whole life without meeting a single Catholic," he said.

"We have them in Bartlett," said W.D. "They're civil enough."

"I dream of the day when I can minister to a larger flock and bring in a greater harvest for the Lord."

W.D. hurried his dinner and left with Lucille as soon as he could. Bidding Joe Smiddick good-bye on the porch, he asked him why the wedding hadn't been in the church.

"There's no heat in the church. It's a summer church."

"So where do you preach in the wintertime?"

"Here in the living room. So in a sense you *were* married in the church." He laughed again.

"But there isn't room for six people in your living room."

"Oh, before you go . . ." The Little Preacher darted back inside and returned with the Marriage Certificate. He held it flat against the wall as W.D. and Lucille signed their names. "I'll get the witnesses to sign when the snow stops."

"Remember," said W.D., "not a word of this to anybody."

"You know me, old friend." They shook hands.

W.D. gave him a ten-dollar bill. "Good-bye then, and thanks." He and Lucille stepped off the porch and hurried to the Oldsmobile.

His old friend called after them, "Come back and visit sometime, you two." The falling snow was thick and silent, muffling his voice.

W.D. made a U-turn in the street, spinning his wheels, and waved to the Little Preacher scarcely visible in his black suit behind the screen.

"Well, Mrs. Nestor," he said, turning to his new wife sitting beside him. She gave him her biggest deep-dimpled smile with tears in her eyes and rode all the way to Rookery with her head on his shoulder.

They stopped again at the trucker's restaurant. W.D. needed to move around in order to relieve the pain across his shoulders caused by straining to see through the falling snow. The same waitress, bringing them coffee, recognized them. She asked if they remembered the fat lady with the fur coat and the little husband.

"We gave them our booth," said Lucille.

"Well, he fell over and died after you left."

"The husband? He died?"

"Fell out of the booth onto the floor." The waitress stepped back as though to make room for the body at her feet. "And the lady got hysterical. She let out a scream that scared hell out of all of us. Sounded like a siren. Even most of the truckers—they think they're so goddam brave—drank up their coffee and cleared out. A couple stayed to do what they could, which wasn't much. I mean, we had quite a time in here. The ambulance was a long time coming."

"Are you sure he was dead?" asked W.D.

"Of course he was dead. He laid on the floor and never moved a muscle. They carted him off to the hospital but he was dead before they ever loaded him up."

"What happened to his wife?" said Lucille.

"Oh, they loaded her up, too. I suppose—" She stopped short when—W.D. noticed—she saw Lucille's wedding ring. She looked stunned. She retired to the cash register to consider (W.D. speculated) the unfairness of this girl and this man married between coffee breaks.

Lucille tried to conceal her weeping as they got back into the car, but there was no hiding tears so copious. With W.D.'s arm around her as they pulled out of the parking lot, she said she couldn't get over the picture in her mind of that man lying dead on the floor and his wife screaming with grief. "Oh, that won't happen to you, will it, Warren? Do you realize that practically every wife I've known has been left behind by a dying husband? I can't stand to think of myself as a widow, Warren. Oh, please, please . . ."

"I'm healthy as an ox," said W.D.

He didn't tell Lucille that despite his reassurances, he considered going no farther until tomorrow. Joe Smiddick had been right about the highways being plowed, but an hour east of Rookery he would have to take an unplowed county road into the river valley. He considered staying with his aunt Nancy in Rookery. Aunt Nancy Clancy, about fifty years old, had survived two husbands, her first being W.D.'s uncle Sherman, and, according to his mother, she was about to marry for the third time. She kept track, by letter, of half a dozen branches of her family. Her second husband had been a banker who'd left her well fixed; she lived in what W.D.'s mother called "a mansion on the best street in town." But how would he explain to Lucille's aunt Velma why they were gone overnight? He pressed on.

Sure enough, the snow in the river valley was up over the front bumper, and several times he had to back up and ram the snow to make any progress. Soon the car's radiator became impacted with snow and the cooling system began to boil. Clouds of steam rose from under the hood. W.D. now knew that they wouldn't make it home by supper time, indeed by bedtime, but of course he didn't let his bride know of his anxiety. "If we can just reach the bridge," he said, "we'll be within four miles of another highway." The steam from the engine grew more intense, blinding him as he weaved along the narrow road between the trees. Finally he reached the bridge, but he could go no farther, couldn't make it up the steep incline out of the valley.

"Bundle up," he told Lucille. "We'll have to find a place to stay."

"Where are we?" she asked.

"Clarkstown."

Clarkstown wasn't officially a town, or even a village; it was a settlement of perhaps thirty people living in the river scrub near this bridge across the Badbattle. There was one place of business in their midst—Ada Lashara's general store.

"I think I see a light in the store," he said. "We'll stop in there and ask for a place."

He expected more tears from Lucille, but she impressed him with her newfound resoluteness in this time of emergency. He would discover this to hold true throughout their married lives, her being strong when the chips were down.

"Let's try the McCurdys," she said. "I was at the McCurdys' once with Sally McCurdy when I was little. Her mother is really nice." So they waded uphill through the thigh-deep snow, past the general store to the McCurdys' house.

❧

SALLY MCCURDY'S MOTHER SAID she was glad to have guests for supper. She seemed to accept without question what W.D. told her, that they were returning from a funeral of a friend in Rookery. Slicing a rubbery carrot into a pot of stew on the black cast-iron cookstove, she said to Lucille, "Last time I had company for a meal was last summer. Ada Lashara and her cousin came up for lunch. Her cousin was fifty, Ada told me later, and on her honeymoon. The cousin and her new husband happened to be driving through Clarkstown and on the spur of the moment decided to pay Ada a call and they stayed with her two nights and two days. They left the husband in charge of the store when they came for lunch. We had the best visit. It seemed like all three of us talked at once the whole time. Ben was off somewhere cutting pulp. That's Sally's daddy. He works away from home more in the summer."

W.D. only vaguely remembered Sally McCurdy, who had been behind him in school, and a year or two ahead of Lucille. Sally had a little brother named Billy who was watching TV in the other room. Ben McCurdy wasn't home and his wife didn't expect him until tomorrow sometime, when the roads would be plowed. W.D. was glad of this. Ben McCurdy by reputation was a hothead. Seated at the kitchen table watching her work, W.D. thought Mrs. McCurdy looked more like a grandmother than the mother of someone as young as Billy. Her straight hair, which she apparently trimmed herself, was short and white and her face and hands were deeply wrinkled. Her baggy brown stockings were covered to below the knee by a green dress she probably bought at an auction. But she had the black snappy eyes of a girl and she smiled easily. "It's too bad it takes a blizzard to bring folks together," she said.

"I remember you from the time Sally invited everybody on the bus to her birthday party," said Lucille. She was distributing four bowls around the table, no two matching and all of them chipped.

"You mean you were here then? What a birthday party that was. I had twenty-three kids, and when the parents came after supper to pick them up there was a traffic jam down at the bridge. Sally was in the fifth or sixth grade."

"I was in fourth," said Lucille. "Do you remember me?"

"Goodness, child, I don't remember anybody who came. All I remember is the shock of seeing the whole string of you coming up the hill from the bus. Sally had told me on her way out that morning that she was inviting somebody over for birthday cake, but I had no idea there would be twenty-three of you. I must have counted you, dearie, but I truly don't remember."

"So often I'll remember something that happened and other people who were there don't recall a thing about it.

Why doesn't everybody remember the same thing, I wonder?"

Mrs. McCurdy stopped working to consider this. "Maybe if we remember something, others don't have to," she said. "You know, I could tell you things about your father that you don't know because you weren't born yet."

"Tell me," said Lucille eagerly. She lowered the lid of the woodbox next to the stove and sat on it.

Mrs. McCurdy blew on a spoonful of stew and, tasting it, she looked down at Lucille. The face of the little girl at the party came back to her. "Oh, I do remember you," she exclaimed. "You sat right there the whole time, while the rest of the partygoers ran and pounced and fought like pups in every room in the house."

"Yes, I remember sitting here and you said to me, 'What's your name, Angel?' and I loved you instantly. I didn't move from this box when it was time to eat. I held my plate and my cake on my lap, and when Aunt Velma came to get me I tried to hide behind the stove and burned my arm. I've always wanted to come back for another visit."

"My heavens, child, why didn't you, in all these years?"

"We only get to Clarkstown once or twice a year, and then only to Ada Lashara's store. We never come up the hill."

"That's no reason. Don't you ever do anything on your own? Doesn't your aunt Velma ever let you out of her sight?"

"Oh, you know how Aunt Velma is. She speaks of you now and again. She says you used to be friends."

"It's true. As girls in school. But that was a hundred years ago. All I know now is that Velma Schuler, like every Schuler before her, has a strong religious streak, and she deserves everyone's respect"—(though she had practically no one's, thought W.D.)—"for raising her brother's girl from infancy. I know what it's like to raise kids single-handed, because Sally and her four brothers, including Billy in there, were brought up with more hindrance than help from their father, and it leaves a woman not much good for anything else. And when I see you grown up and pretty as a picture and friendly and setting the table like you've done it before, well, I have to believe your aunt Velma is a mighty good soul."

After a respectful silence, Lucille said, "So you knew my dad."

"Of course I did. We lived neighbors to your farm when I was a little tyke, and I remember the day your grandparents took the three of us little ones into town. Your father, your aunt Velma, and me. We were all about the same age. I suppose they were going shopping and just happened to have us on their hands. Well, your grandfather no more than parked the car in front of the drugstore when his cousin Sarah Bishop looked into the backseat and said, 'My, aren't these Schuler children the little lovelies.' I remember that's the word she used, lovelies, and she put her head in the window to give your father and your aunt Velma a kiss. I was clear across the seat and out of danger. And Velma gave old Sarah a kiss and a little hug, and when it was your father's turn, he bit the poor woman on the nose. Sarah gave out a little scream and pulled her head out and went trotting down the street holding her nose."

Mrs. McCurdy laughed but Lucille did not. Lucille looked stunned, probably (thought W.D.) because she'd never before heard a story about her father. All she knew about him—and therefore all W.D. knew—was that after his parents died, he spent long periods away from home, nobody knew where, leaving the farmwork to his sister, Velma, who eventually sold off the livestock and rented out most of the land to neighbors. At first, hungover, he returned to the farm periodically for a few days of rest and repentance, but he hadn't been back now for seventeen years, not since the time he showed up with a year-old baby girl he called Lucy. That time he stayed only overnight and left alone before dawn.

As Mrs. McCurdy served supper and called Billy to the table, W.D. made a brief call home to report his whereabouts, but of course Lucille couldn't do that. How would she explain her presence in Clarkstown? While eating, W.D. wondered if maybe their being gone overnight would cause Lucille to give up their secret. He hoped so. The sooner the world knew they were married, the sooner they could go to bed together. Maybe even tonight they could be man and wife. Sitting across from his pretty new spouse, watching the muscles of her face working over the tough pieces of stew beef, he raised himself to a state of erotic expectation which he had to overcome after supper when he heard her on the phone, out of Mrs. McCurdy's earshot, lying to her aunt Velma. She claimed to have been kept so late at band practice that she was snowbound, and that she was staying overnight at the home of her home-ec teacher, Mrs. Wright. W.D. was shocked at the ease with which she told this falsehood. Was this the Lucille he'd known since he was ten, the same girl who'd cried two years ago when he described the day he'd spent with his father castrating piglets? Had he overestimated her innocence?

No, he hadn't. Although they never in their forty-some-year marriage discussed this unsettling moment, Lucille turned out to be exactly the woman he thought she was, quiet, pliable, unassuming, and innocent—except where her aunt Velma was concerned. In her surrogate mother's company, Lucille was submissive but only up to a point. Nosy as Velma Schuler was, she couldn't extract information that Lucille wanted to withhold.

Sitting now on the bench in his side yard under the burr oak, W.D. recalled the time Lucille almost made him laugh with her quick comeback to her aunt Velma. It was Easter Sunday and they picked up Velma, as usual, on their way to church, and Lucille was wearing for the first time the expensive coat that she wore for eight or ten years thereafter. Lucille had picked it out at the Sears store in Rookery, and W.D. paid forty-some dollars for it. As they watched Velma come out her back door that morning, W.D. said to Lucille, "She'll want to know what your coat cost us," and Lucille replied, "I know it, she's such a skinflint." And sure enough the first thing she did upon getting into the backseat was to bend forward and feel the fabric of the collar and say, "I bet this cost a pretty penny." "It cost a dollar," said Lucille, "at the Salvation Army Store."

W.D. had to smile at the memory and was given a curious look by Kermit, who happened to be passing by on his riding lawnmower. He regretted the smile, because Kermit was sure to tattle to Viola and she would ask him what was going on in his head. And sure enough, later, at supper, his daughter said, "Kermit said you was setting out there with a shit-eating grin on your face, Pops. What was you grinning at?" Although W.D. considered this sort of question an invasion of privacy, he decided to tell them about the coat and Aunt Velma. If he didn't, Viola would worry the subject to death. But neither his daughter nor his son-in-law saw anything funny in the story, and they gave each other the conspiratorial look W.D. hated.

He spent the rest of the meal recalling the night at McCurdy's, how cozy and warm it was, with the night turning colder as the snow stopped falling, with the furnace clicking on every ten minutes through the night, with his bride sleeping in the room next to his.

The following day school started at noon, and the snowplow got to Clarkstown just in time for W.D. to get her there. Aunt Velma never found out they were married until after graduation. Lucille told her over the phone after she'd moved in with W.D. and his mother. (W.D. had made two trips with her things when Velma was at church.) She didn't do anything about it, didn't even put up a fuss. As Lucille said, her aunt was too smart to believe she could keep her home forever.

4

✦

ABOUT TWENTY-FIVE YEARS LATER, W.D. was once
again snowbound overnight in Clarkstown. This happened during the last of his eight years as a bus driver for
the Bartlett school district—a job he finally quit because his
livestock didn't seem to approve of it.

In order to reach Clarkstown by seven a.m. and pick up
his first passenger, W.D. had to be up and dressed each
morning at 4:15 and tend to his cows before dawn. He found
that whenever school vacations allowed him to milk them as
the sun was coming up, the animals were docile, but on
school days, in the yellow light of electric bulbs under the
dark hayloft, with the barn radio playing Whoopee John
polkas, they would continually shift and sidle as far as their
stanchions would allow as W.D. came at them with the tubes
and cups of the milking machine. It was no use asking Sonny
to help him because Sonny refused to get out of bed before
the morning was half gone.

After milking he would start his bus and hurry back to
the barn to pitch a half-dozen forkfuls of hay down from the

loft while the engine warmed, filling the yard with a billowing cloud of exhaust. Then, carrying his thermos of coffee and chewing on something left over from supper, he boarded his bus and settled into the driver's seat, where he sipped coffee and listened to the engine until the frost on the windshield melted away. Then he switched on the headlights, shifted gears, and set off across the prairie and down through the scrub to Clarkstown.

All this for Willy McCurdy. Eleven years ago, Willy McCurdy, a grandson of Mrs. McCurdy, had been a runny-nosed and bewildered first grader pulled off and on the bus by a couple of long-legged older brothers. Mrs. McCurdy seemed glad to have this houseful of grandchildren, for as they piled into the bus she would stand at the window and wave at W.D. Now Willy was seventeen and Clarkstown's only scholar—and a reluctant one at that. As often as not W.D. pulled up to the McCurdy house (where W.D. and Lucille had spent their wedding night) and honked his horn on a day that Willy had chosen to stay home. This made Mrs. McCurdy ashamed. What made it immediately clear that Willy was skipping school was the absence of her face in the window. Whenever this happened, W.D. would tip his head to the side and mutter, "That kid ought to be told how much gasoline is wasted on him over a year's time. He ought to be taught respect for the people who are trying to educate him. He ought to quit school." Then he would make a U-turn and head back up through the scrub with an empty bus. It took him twenty minutes to reach his second stop, the Erickson farm.

Now, in the late afternoon of a heavy snowfall, the bus

was swallowed by the scrub as it began its winding descent to the river. "You picked a mighty poor day to go to school," W.D. said over his shoulder to Willy, his only remaining passenger. He had to step on the gas to make headway downhill through the snow, and he wasn't certain he could climb back out of the valley until the road was plowed. The deep snow billowed up over the fenders like water at the prow of a ship, and at each curve of the road W.D. was momentarily blinded as he turned into the billow. He put his windshield wipers to work against the spray of snow that fell on the warm glass and melted.

"I had to go, Grandpa was sober this morning." Willy said this into W.D.'s ear, for he was sitting directly behind him and leaning forward on the chrome handrail. As always Willy was watching him drive. "I never saw it where you had to give her gas downhill before."

"Like driving through molasses," said W.D. "I don't believe we'd even be moving if I didn't have chains on." He'd hesitated at the Erickson driveway, after letting off the giggling flock of Erickson girls, and considered taking Willy back to Bartlett instead of driving into the valley ahead of the snowplow. Now he wished he'd turned back.

"You going to try to make it back to town?" asked Willy.

"If I can stay in the tracks I'm making, I might make it, but I don't know where I'll turn around. Will the plow be out here tonight?"

"Hard to say. We're a long ways from anywhere."

They covered another mile in silence, until they came to a jack pine lying across the road, having been snapped off by the weight of the wet snow. Willy, without being told, jumped off the bus and tugged at the tree until there was enough room for the bus to pass. Watching him in the head-lights, W.D. was surprised at how much snow had fallen—Willy, taller than W.D., was in it up to his thighs, and each step was an effort.

Willy got back on board and peeled the wet snow from his pant legs.

"You're wet to the crotch," said W.D.

"Cold, too," said Willy, digging caked snow out of his shoes.

A mile farther on, W.D. noticed steam rising from under the hood. "We're boiling," he muttered. "Radiator's packed with snow."

Willy suggested, "We got a extra bed. We can walk from here, it's only a mile."

"It would seem like a hundred in snow this deep. I can make it to the bridge before she boils dry."

Ahead through the trees and the twilight they caught glimpses of the frozen, snow-covered Badbattle lying flat as a slab. A few yards short of the bridge W.D. switched off the engine and said, "Here's where we stop." Turning on the dome light to read his watch he added, "Milking time."

Willy led the way across the bridge, breaking a trail with his long, high-stepping legs. When he reached the other side, he stopped and waited for W.D., who was finding it difficult to lift his foot knee-high with each step. They stood together for a few moments while W.D. caught his breath and scanned the darkness. A single streetlight hung over the road ahead. After rubbing his cheeks to warm them, he felt the touch of snow on his face. "Wind's picking up," he said. "Let's go."

They had gone only a few feet when a sudden blast of blinding snow forced them to turn and trudge sideways with their faces averted. Clarkstown's only streetlight, a bare bulb suspended between two power poles, guided them up the sloping road to the first building, an abandoned store. Leaning against the lee wall for shelter, W.D. was so exhausted that he didn't know if he could make it to Willy's house. The road climbed through the forested hillside to a small plateau where several houses were grouped in a clearing, and it was at this upper level that the McCurdy house stood. Here, at the first flat spot above the river, among a few abandoned buildings known as downtown, stood Ada Lashara's general store.

"Do you suppose the store is open?" he asked.

"It's always open."

Willy led the way across the street toward the storefront with a short tube of red neon flickering over the door. In the swirling snow, the neon created a rosy nimbus around Willy.

"My grandpa's probably in here," he said, holding the door open for W.D.

The place was stuffed with merchandise. Narrow aisles twisted between tubs and counters and racks. Suspended from the ceiling at several points were flowerpots from which hung a profusion of dusty-leafed philodendron vines. It was too dark around the walls to see what the high shelving contained, but here and there a bottle or a can reflected light from the back of the store. W.D. started for the light and stepped on the tail of a cat that screeched and ran.

Willy laughed and called, "Ada."

"Yeah, back here," said a high, cracking voice.

"They're back by the stove," said Willy.

They made their way past a counter where the clothing department overlapped with the bread and pastry section so that dozens of packaged donuts were partially covered by a pile of striped overalls; past a shelf of canned goods including beans, tuna, and motor oil; and around a candy rack draped with neckties. Fire glowed in the wood-burning stove, which stood with its door open under a light hanging from the high ceiling. There in a semicircle sat Ada Lashara, the proprietor, in a rocking chair, together with Willy's grandfather and a very old man whose face was almost hidden behind a long white beard and a profusion of sidewhiskers. The two men occupied a couple of old easy chairs. An empty chair stood beside Willy's grandfather.

"Who's that you brought with you, Willy?" said his grandfather, peering into the shadows.

"Land sakes," said Ada Lashara from the rocking chair. "It's the school bus driver." She was small and arthritic and wrapped in a patched black sweater. By rocking back and forth very fast, and with the help of the chair's momentum, she got to her feet and snatched at the cuff of W.D.'s jacket with a gnarled hand. Her shoulders were permanently hunched up to her ears and her back was bent so that she could look up at his face only by turning her head sideways. "Your wife phoned twice. My, but don't you look like a couple of snowmen. The phone's over here on the wall."

She led W.D. over to a shadowy corner and with a broom from a nearby display she brushed snow off the legs of his jeans while he dialed home. Hearing a busy signal, he hung up and returned to the stove, Ada following with the broom.

"Looks like I'm stuck in Clarkstown," he said, holding his hands out to the warm fire.

The younger man in the chair surprised him by answering, "Think nothing of it, I've been stuck here for sixty-six years."

"This here's Ben McCurdy," said Ada, now sweeping snow off Willy. "And this is . . ."

W.D. didn't catch the old man's name. Shaking hands with McCurdy he said, "So you're Willy's grandfather."

"I'm grandpa to Willy and some of his brothers," he said, getting slowly to his foot. "Willy's the only one left home." Ben McCurdy was lean and tall, and he seemed to get taller as he unfolded himself.

"I know that," said W.D., looking up at his drink-ravaged face. "And he's the only student left in Clarkstown." He felt snow melting in his eyebrows and he wiped them with the back of his hand. "In fact, he's my only passenger east of the Erickson place."

Ben McCurdy was drunk. He tipped slowly forward, then caught himself as he said, "And he's the only son of a bitch on the river who doesn't know a chainsaw from a wristwatch."

"Now Ben," said Ada, returning to her rocking chair. "He's your grandson and I won't have you—"

"What I said stands," he shouted, tipping forward again.

W.D., trying to change the subject, turned to the old man and asked his name.

"Stone deaf," said Ben McCurdy. "Don't make a speck of difference what his name is, he can't hear nothing."

"Guess I'll try the telephone again," said W.D., returning

to the shadowy corner. He heard his home phone ringing. Waiting for Lucille to answer, he heard the low, steady howl of the wind blowing over the chimney, and the staccato puffs of dancing flames. He heard a scratching noise behind the flour sacks, which was quickly silenced by the thud of the pouncing cat.

Lucille was relieved to hear from him, to know he was safe. She, with their son and daughter's help, had milked the cows.

"Lu, you shouldn't even have to step foot in the barn. Sonny knows the ropes out there."

"Oh, you know Sonny."

"I know, I know. Lu . . ." Thoughts of his lazy son always made W.D. tongue-tied. He wanted to tell her that she was spoiling him, that Sonny would never learn to do a decent day's work as long as she was around to help him with every little chore, but he'd already said this to her umpteen times, and besides, Ada and Ben McCurdy and Willy were listening. He dropped the subject, said good-bye, and returned to the circle of light.

The old man with the beard was speaking. "I never held it against Swedes that they couldn't learn English," he said in a surprisingly strong and melodious voice. "Every Swede I knew was a dependable man, yessir, a dependable man. Syl Hendrum was a Swede, nor was he ever ashamed of it. Hendrum could saw more timber than any man in camp."

At first, because of Ben McCurdy's mean reputation, W.D. was relieved to see that he'd fallen asleep in his chair, his head back and his mouth open, but then he had a disquieting thought: What if Sonny turned out to be as worthless as Ben McCurdy? They already shared the same sullen, brooding, angry nature. Sonny was lazy, like this man, simply refusing to do any chores around the farm except feed the chickens and gather eggs, which was women's work. Sonny was eighteen, supposedly a senior in high school, two years older than his sister Viola, and yet Viola could work circles around Sonny.

"Hendrum never stood out with the axe," the old man continued, "but just get into big timber and put Hendrum on one end of a saw and watch him outlast two men. That's right, I seen it where they had to bring in a third man on the other end of the saw, and Hendrum wouldn't even be slowed down. Made no difference, oak or pine, he cut it like cheese. It had to do with his build, don't you see. He was a small, stoop-shouldered man, so the sawing position was natural to him. They claimed he kept a Testament under his mattress to read out of when he had a spare minute."

Willy started to speak, but Ada raised her hand to stop him, allowing no one to break in on the old man's monologue. What did she care about axes, saws, and pike poles, about bunkhouses, log chains, horse-drawn skids? W.D. himself didn't care, and he suspected that Ada didn't either, but he understood her need to listen. There was something so natural and soothing about the old man's voice, like the sound of nesting birds or the rustle of dry oak leaves, that he wanted it to go on and on. He heard it as one hears river current bubbling around a rock, a pleasing sound one might listen to all one's life without knowing what it meant.

"Whether Hendrum kept a Testament was an argument I

never entered into. But I will say it wasn't likely. I never heard of a praying Swede, much less a reading one."

The old man paused, and Willy cleared his throat, but Ada, apparently accustomed to the rhythm of these monologues, raised her hand again for the old man's concluding statement:

"Besides, if he had a Testament it must have been printed in Swede, and you can't call that reading."

Ada lowered her hand and Willy spoke softly, while looking at his grandfather with trepidation. "Let's go up to the house."

"What did your wife say?" Ada asked W.D.

"Said everything's blown shut. The snow blows right in behind the plows. No more plowing till daylight, and then only if the snow lets up and the wind dies down."

"Is that all?" said Ada, obviously starved for news.

"My cows are milked." W.D. felt suddenly very hungry, and he nudged Willy, who had dropped a stream of spit on the top of the stove and was watching it sizzle.

"Anything else?" asked Ada.

"That's all," said W.D., leading Willy through the shadows toward the front door.

"I expect we'll see you in the morning," called Ada. "Come back in the morning and set a while."

The wind was colder now, and their wet jackets and pants quickly froze and rubbed like armor as they walked. If Ben McCurdy hadn't looked settled for the night, W.D. might have bought something edible from Ada and spent the night in the third easy chair, but he didn't fancy sleeping next to a mean drunk. He said, "You're sure I won't be putting your grandmother to any trouble?"

"No trouble," said Willy. "She'll be glad of the company. She'll fix us a hot meal."

Gusts of snow swirled at them from every direction and the darkness was complete. Willy stepped off the road and disappeared into a ditch. He would have climbed the wrong bank and found himself in the woods if W.D.'s shouts hadn't brought him back to the road. To prevent losing each other, W.D. took off his scarf and gave an end to Willy, and the second time Willy stumbled into the ditch he pulled W.D. with him. After this they tried walking in the ditch with the bank on either side to guide them, but here the snow was deeper, for the moving snow, like water, was filling in the low spots and W.D. had trouble putting his feet in Willy's tracks.

Nearing the plateau, W.D. was so exhausted that he considered letting go of the scarf and following the ditch later when his energy returned. Five more steps he told himself; then on the fifth step he challenged himself to another five; then several more sets of five until, stumbling and falling forward on his face, he let go. In a minute, as soon as my breath returns, I will stand up and go forward, he told himself, but until then I cannot move. Now if I winked an eye I would die of the effort, but as soon as my breath returns . . . Why doesn't my breath return?

It suddenly occurred to him that he was smothering face-down in the snow. He was taken by the same silent panic that he remembered from childhood when, more asleep than awake, he sensed that he was bound tightly in his twisted bedclothes. His chest was about to explode and his mind twirled dizzily. He pulled his legs up under him and rose rump-first to his hands and knees. He ravenously breathed the air of the hollow he had made in the snow, his shoulders heaving over his head like a vomiting dog. He was scarcely twenty yards from the McCurdys' house. Willy had gone in for a flashlight and he came out with his grandmother and they helped him inside.

Mrs. McCurdy and Willy were proud of the bathroom they had recently remodeled, and they encouraged him to take a bath. He soaked in the tub for half an hour, and was given a change of clothes from Ben McCurdy's room. When he emerged for dinner—beef stew again—he felt restored, except for a tremor in his hands caused by his close encounter with death. He was still shaky driving home the next day, but he ignored it and eventually it went away.

5

❖

BECAUSE NEITHER KERMIT nor Viola trusted him with the Buick, W.D. drove the International into Bartlett. The old truck hadn't been out of the yard for years and it bucked and roared and laid a trail of smoke along the highway. At Bartlett's only stoplight, W.D. became flustered and stepped on the gas and the brake at the same time and the truck jerked across the intersection and the engine died. When he got it started again and let up on the brake, he shot through town to the fairgrounds, where he stopped behind the grandstand. In front of the grandstand was an oval track for horse racing and within the track was a Little League baseball diamond. A man about W.D.'s age was raking smooth the dirt around home plate, and W.D. asked him what the track measured. "It measures four hundred forty yards, a quarter mile," said the man, lifting his cap and wiping the sweat off his bald scalp with his shirtsleeve. "It's for horseracing at fair time."

"I know it. I haven't missed a county fair since seventy-eight. I was into cattle more in those days—cows and a few pigs. I can't remember why, but I completely missed the fair of seventy-eight. You know my place out along the highway. Four miles west. Turkeys now."

"Yeah, I know your place. You're the runner."

"Every day a mile. Except in the winter. I can't breathe a lot of cold air."

"My wife's brother was the same way. He died finally. Pneumonia."

W.D. stepped over and laid his cap on the front bench of the grandstand and began to run clockwise around the track. The man dropped his rake and followed him, first at a quick, self-conscious walk, then at a trot. He was a smooth runner, his head bent forward as though to ram the atmosphere and his arms churning in perfect circles, like the driving rods on a locomotive. W.D. said "Hey!" as the man passed him, but the man, paying no attention, broke into a sprint and lost his cap. He ran as fast as he could to a point halfway around the track, then he slowed to a jog, then he walked, then he tipped over and collapsed on the grass beside the track.

W.D. turned the man over on his back and said, "You can't run a mile full tilt." The man's belly heaved and his face was the color of a carrot. W.D. heard voices and looked across the field to see an orange school bus beside the grandstand letting out a crowd of small boys in baseball uniforms. After a few minutes the bald man was able to draw himself up to a sitting position and he sat at W.D.'s feet, drawing quick breaths. Another bus arrived and a crowd of boys in green uniforms merged with the others, raising the pitch of young voices to a level that sounded to W.D. like feeding time in the turkey lot. At home plate a man in sunglasses was waving papers in the air and pointing in all directions. Several women, mothers probably, climbed into the grandstand, and as the players sorted themselves out, the whites in the field and the greens up to bat, W.D. heard the women shouting their support. The first batter came to the plate and one woman shouted, "Come on now, Jerry," and another, "Hey, Rodney, bean the puny bastard." The centerfielder for the whites, with FARMER'S CO-OP stitched on the back of his shirt, kept turning around to look at the two old men behind him, one sitting on the grass, the other standing beside him.

"I believe I'm all right now," said the bald man and he got to his feet.

"You go back the way you came and pick up your hat," said W.D. "I'll continue on around."

As he approached the nearly empty grandstand, the women's voices carried clearly down to him: "Who is that old fart running?"

"Yeah, what does he think he's doing? Look at his overalls."

"That's old man Nestor. Viola Kilbride's father. I wonder if she knows he's in town."

"Has he lost his mind?"

"Somebody really ought to phone Viola."

W.D. sat down next to his cap to rest. A fat boy, the catcher for the white team, squatted in front of him. On his back it said, HARVEST BAR. The batter was a very small boy whose green shirt hung on his narrow shoulders like drapery and whose wrists were no larger than the handle of his bat. On his back it said, CHARLIE'S SHOES. The umpire, the man in dark glasses, stood behind the pitcher and called the first pitch a strike. The women in the grandstand muttered.

W.D. heard one of them say, "What's a runt like that doing in the lineup?" CHARLIE'S SHOES swung at the second pitch after it was in the catcher's mitt, and the women called to him, "Come on, Charlie's Shoes, you haven't had a hit all summer." "You always swing too late." "Pull up your pants." Strike three. The women shouted more scornful remarks.

CHARLIE'S SHOES picked up his glove and walked out to the outfield, drawing his shoulders up to his ears, obviously trying to blend into the grass. The voice of one of the women echoed off the roof of the grandstand and rolled out across the fairgrounds: "As long as you're out for baseball, Charlie's Shoes, we'll never win a goddam game."

❖

IN EARLY NOVEMBER it wasn't yet supper time when daylight died. W.D. and Kermit stood watching the last truckload of turkeys pull out of the yard, a mixture of rain and snow falling through the beam of its headlights. Kermit said, "A harvest of six thousand seven hundred and forty-three birds may not be our best year ever, but we've had worse. It will see us comfortable through the winter and then some. Next year without the sickness, we'll be up over seven thousand again, wait and see." Although payment wouldn't arrive for several days it already cast Kermit into a rare mood of fellow-feeling. He turned to his father-in-law and added, "How does a hot brandy sound about now? I've saved a pint of brandy for the occasion, so we'll go in and get into some warm clothes and have ourselves a hot brandy before supper." He clapped his hand on W.D.'s shoulder, which, even through his jacket, felt bony and small.

"I'll be right in," said W.D. "I'm going to check the lot for strays."

He went through the gate to the dark field and began to run. The four lights that burned at the corners of the lot all summer to discourage thieves and coyotes were off now. He hadn't run for weeks, and his hips and knees felt stiff and painful. The snow thickened and fell in big flakes that blinded him. He gave up and walked back to the house. He paused at the kitchen door, dreading the winter ahead, spending day after day indoors with Kermit and Viola. He grieved as never before for Lucille, who'd been content to spend the snowy evenings sitting beside him on the couch, watching videos from the library and listening to W.D.'s commentary. Kermit and Viola spent their days and nights watching stupid talk shows and sitcoms with the volume turned up so loud you'd think they were deaf.

Standing there in the wet snowfall, he allowed himself an unusual thought: He guessed he must have loved Lucille. Yes, he loved her, though he'd never told her. What was the joke about the Norwegian? He loved his wife so much he told her? The day he heard the crowd at the pool hall laugh at that, he decided he'd tell Lucille he loved her. But the opportunity never presented itself before she got Alzheimer's and didn't even know who he was. Which was okay, because it saved him the embarrassment of having to utter those unfamiliar words and surely she knew it anyhow. Sometimes in the evening, watching TV, he and Lucille held hands.

❖

WITHIN A WEEK, feeling cooped up beyond endurance, he drove the truck to town in the late afternoon, and parked in front of the public library. He went in and felt good about how nothing had changed; the woman at the desk was the same woman on duty three years ago, the videos were on the same shelves against the north wall, a couple of students sat as before at a table copying out of encyclopedias. One of the students, a boy, looked familiar, but W.D. couldn't remember where he'd seen him.

On the video shelves he found a wealth of new material. He chose a three-cassette biography of Winston Churchill and took it downstairs to the viewing room. The room was small, partitioned off with glass walls from the children's section. He'd previewed a few videos down here over the years, but he'd never sat down to watch an entire show. He didn't enjoy it. He was surprised to discover that he didn't like being alone. Running was different. Running alone allowed your mind to wander, allowed you to talk to yourself whenever you felt the need, but watching TV didn't work that way. Watching TV, you needed somebody beside you, like Lucille, to make comments to. After the first cassette he switched off the monitor and went home in despair. Waking up the next morning, he remembered where he'd seen the boy who looked so familiar sitting at the library table. He'd seen him at the fairgrounds. He was the inept baseball player, Charlie's Shoes.

Later that week, for diversion, W.D. returned to the library for two more afternoons and watched the rest of the Churchill biography. Both days he saw Charlie's Shoes upstairs. He hoped to get used to sitting alone in the viewing room but didn't, not even when he became absorbed in

Churchill's funeral. What interested him most was the transporting of the great man's body by ship from the cathedral to his burial upriver, and the way the huge cranes along the shoreline dipped as the ship passed. He turned to tell Lucille how wonderful it was to see these gigantic machines bowing like human beings in respect, how the men at the controls had to coordinate this—but of course Lucille wasn't there.

Well, he had to tell somebody. He hurried upstairs and found the librarian busy at the checkout counter. He went over to the boy's table and, leaning over him, panting, said, "You're Charlie's Shoes, am I right? The baseball player?"

The little boy looked up from his pencil, obviously pleased to be known as an athlete. He said, "Yep," and then added, to be truthful, "But I'm not very good."

"Well, I just saw the damnedest thing downstairs on a video." He didn't lower his voice, and as he described the cranes dippping along the river as Churchill's body passed, he became aware that he was also addressing three or four other people at the reading tables. "Come down and see for yourselves," he said, heading back to the stairway. "I'll back it up and show that part over again."

At the viewing room he discovered he had only one follower, Charlie's Shoes. The boy looked up at him expectantly with innocent eyes. W.D. thought him handsome and guessed he was ten years old.

"Come in and sit down," he said, seating himself and pointing at the remaining chairs in the viewing room.

The boy, having evidently been warned against getting too cozy with strangers, remained in the doorway and said, "That's okay, I'll watch it from out here."

"All right, suit yourself." W.D. rewound the tape partway and watched the funeral again. He turned and was pleased to see the boy in the doorway, staring at the screen with his mouth open, obviously fascinated. When he got to the part he was waiting for, he explained how the crane operator moved the levers to get his machine to do that human thing, and then it was over.

"Well, what did you think of that?" he asked, shutting down the video player and the TV.

"Who's the dead guy?" said the boy.

"That was Winston Churchill."

"It wasn't in color."

"No, this was a long time ago, before color."

"I didn't see any birds."

"Birds? What birds?"

"Cranes."

Oh, boy, this kid didn't know any more about machinery than Lucille. As he explained the difference between the bird and the machine, Charlie's Shoes came into the room and sat down next to him. Nodding at everything he was told, he struck W.D. as very intelligent. But he'd never heard of Winston Churchill. So W.D. told him about the great man, together with a summary of World War II, and when he finished the lecture the boy made no move to leave.

"Well, I guess we ought to go," W.D. prompted.

The boy rose obediently from his chair and said, "Can we come back tomorrow and watch it again?"

"Oh, I suppose," said W.D., pleased beyond words.

❖

THROUGHOUT THE WINTER, every time W.D. went to the library, Charlie's Shoes was there waiting for him, and they went downstairs and watched videos. When they saw W.D.'s old favorites, like Jacques Cousteau underwater and Ernie Kovacs, he did a lot of explaining. One day between videos, it occurred to him to ask the boy why he spent so much time at the library.

Shrugging, the boy replied, "I like it here."

"But don't you have any friends to play with?"

"They're all at basketball practice after school."

"How come you're not?"

"I'm rotten at basketball." The boy paused and then added, as though quoting a parent or a coach, "I'm not athletically inclined."

Upon further questioning he revealed, to W.D.'s amazement, that he'd never enjoyed running.

"I run a mile a day, except in winter."

"A whole mile?"

W.D. nodded. "It's good for the system. You ought to try it."

The boy shivered, as though chilled by the thought, and shook his head.

At the beginning of *Brideshead Revisited* the boy exclaimed, "Hey, that's Jeremy Irons," and W.D. corrected him, saying, "No, that's Charles Ryder."

Each day, when they were finished watching, W.D. gave the boy, who lived about six blocks away, a ride home through the dusky, snowy streets. One late afternoon, when the truck stopped in front of his small house on Fir Street and the noisy engine subsided to an idling growl, the boy asked W.D. what his name was. "W. D. Nestor," he replied.

"No, I mean what do the letters stand for?"

"They stand for two names I never cared for."

"What are they?"

W.D. gave him a haughty look as though he'd never before encountered such impertinence, but then he relented. "My name is Warren, named after my dad."

"How about the 'D'?"

"Darrell, named after nobody. My mother just liked the name."

"My name is Kevin Luuya."

"Luuya." Warren had heard the name. "Is your daddy the preacher Luuya?"

"Yep, Fourth Street Congregational."

"And your mama ran off with the rock star."

"She did?"

The boy looked shaken, and W.D. guessed he shouldn't have spoken about his mother. He changed the subject:

"Now don't let me catch you calling me anything but W.D., you hear?"

"I won't," said the boy, getting out of the truck. Today, as usual, W.D. waited in the truck while the boy took a key out of his pocket, unlocked the door to the dark house, and turned on a light inside.

Driving home, he recalled what he knew of the Luuyas, a family of Finlanders who began as small farmers not far from W.D.'s place. The preacher's father had been W.D.'s age and they had known each other in country school. The preacher's father had a kind of half-wit brother called Dusty, who ran a garbage route in Staggerford, which was only seven miles west of Bartlett, and who died of heart failure several years ago. The boy Kevin's mother had been Susie Nesbitt before she married the preacher, and all the Nesbitt girls were said to be a little on the wild side. W.D. remembered the scandal when Susie hooked up with a rock guitarist who performed one night at the Berrington County Fair. She ran off to Texas with him, so people said. Just up and left the preacher high and dry with a young son to bring up.

And what was the preacher himself up to these days, that he should never be home at supper time when the boy came from the library? W.D., who fancied himself a pretty fair judge of character, decided to check the man out—an easy thing to accomplish. All he had to do was take in a service at Fourth Street Congregational.

It was a cold, snowy Sunday when he showed up for church. The sign out front said the preacher, Ollie Luuya, would be speaking today about LOSING THINGS. Inside, a loud furnace blower switched itself on and off every few minutes, but still it was chilly and W.D. was glad he'd put on his long underwear. Sitting in a back pew, he counted twenty-five parishioners scattered around the church. He saw that one of them, sitting up front, was the boy. When the preacher came out into the sanctuary, W.D. recognized him as someone he'd seen around town without knowing who he was. He had a full head of gray hair, a commanding voice, and an authoritative way of gesturing and moving about. He wore a brown choir robe. The service consisted of four hymns sung by the congregation and endless biblical passages read by the preacher. W.D. covered his eyes and slept until it was over.

"W. D. Nestor," he said, introducing himself in the cold vestibule.

"Nestor, W. D. Nestor, I've heard that name somewhere."

"Maybe from your son. We go to the library together."

"That's it, yes indeed, you're the man Kevin talks about, the man with the old truck. Well, well, welcome to our humble little . . ."

Reverend Luuya was interrupted by an elderly woman tugging at the sleeve of his robe who wanted to comment on the flowerless altar. W.D. waited, thinking the preacher would have more to say to him, but he didn't. He just kept greeting others as they came up to him and shook his hand. Finally, when only W.D and the boy were left standing in the vestibule, the preacher turned to them and said, while unbuttoning his robe, "So I suppose you two are off to the library." When his son told him the library was closed on Sundays, W.D. was distinctly aware of a look of disappointment crossing the man's face. This told him all he wanted to know about Ollie Luuya. He was a minister so wrapped up in his ministry that he had no time for his son. Testing him further, W.D. asked the boy if he'd like to shoot some pool. In this day and age you didn't let your child go off with someone you didn't know very well. The boy said yes, and the minister gave them a distracted smile and headed for the sanctuary, straightening hymnals in their holders as he went. W.D. drove the boy to the pool hall, bought a beer for himself and a Coke for his guest, and taught him how to play eight ball.

Over the next eight years they played pool at least once a week, sometimes two or three times a week during school vacations, and they continued to check the library for new videos. W. D. was surprised by how fond he became of Kevin. The boy was on his mind day and night the way Lucille used to be. Then, at the age of eighteen, Kevin Luuya went into the army for two years, and W.D. missed him so much he wrote him three or four postcards. He wrote mostly about the turkeys and the weather. He never mentioned Viola or Kermit, who'd begun talking about spending their winters in Florida. Kevin responded with a couple of newsy letters about boot camp, but after that he wrote nothing.

6

✦

WATER SPARKLED SO BRIGHT on the highway that W.D.,
sitting by the window, couldn't keep his mind on the
weekly *Bartlett World*. Snowbanks diminished before his
eyes, uncovering patches of brown grass, and the old red oak
in the front yard, having hung on to its leaves through fierce
winter winds, released them now to a puff of warm air from
the south.

"I'm going to see Nancy Clancy," he called from his chair.

This winter had been the worst of the eighty-two he'd
lived through. Day after day the north wind had sucked a
small, stinging snow out of a sky so hopelessly gray that the
barn cats, even the pretty ones, put on shaggy, dull coats and
Viola's new black Labrador was content to lie for hours on
rugs, moving only his eyes and the end of his tail. It seemed
to W.D. that the only break in the overcast sky had been the
bitter stretch in January when the air itself froze and he
couldn't see across the highway through the icy haze until
the sun burned through at noon and raised the temperature
to twenty-five below. For over two months he had been con-

174

fined to the house. He had lost his patience early, and then he lost his impatience, reconciling himself to a daily schedule reduced to three activities: smoking his pipe; eating the sandwiches Kevin Luuya prepared for him; and reading the weekly paper over and over, forgetting each paragraph as he went on to the next. His days became so simple and shadowless that he couldn't remember one from another, and it wasn't until this morning's sudden thaw—the last day of his life—that he remembered Nancy Clancy. Old plans, set aside years ago, were worth considering once more.

"I'm going to see Nancy Clancy," he said again, his voice rumbling with phlegm. Into the living room came Kevin Luuya, wiping his hands on a towel. He was twenty, discharged from the army and staying with W.D. for forty-five dollars a week while Viola and Kermit wintered in Florida.

"Who's Nancy Clancy?" he said.

"My aunt Nancy. We used to visit her every so often."

"Who did?"

"My brother and I. My cousins. She lives in Rookery."

"I didn't know you had a brother." Nor did he believe it. Kermit had claimed the old guy was growing senile. Kevin scarcely knew him after being away two years. It was incredible how quickly W.D. was failing.

"Mind you. I'm going to see her," he insisted.

"All right. We'll plan a day."

"This afternoon," he said. "I'm going after lunch." When he saw Kevin turn to look at him sternly, he took his pipe from the pocket of his vest and examined the crusty bowl. He hadn't smoked much in his lifetime, but he'd taken it up seriously at the age of eighty, figuring he'd be soon dead anyhow.

"I'm supposed to see the employment office this afternoon," said Kevin. "I won't have time."

"I'll take the truck."

"Don't be silly."

"I'll take the truck."

"You're not up to it. You haven't been out all winter."

W.D. blew into the stem of his pipe until spit bubbled in the bowl.

"Oh, all right," said Kevin, who wasn't eager to find a job anyhow. This duty was fine with him. Sit around the farmhouse all day, make a couple sandwiches for lunch, a couple more for dinner, feed the dog, watch TV. The only trouble was that his old friend W.D. wasn't the same man he'd been before Kevin went into the army. He was silent and curmudgeonly. Seeing him like this was enough to put you off old people.

After their sandwiches, it took Kevin fifteen minutes to transfer W.D. from his chair by the window out to the car. First stop was the coat closet. Kevin said, "You don't need your overcoat. It's a spring day."

"Tut," said the old man. He carefully crossed his white scarf over his throat and struggled into his black overcoat while Kevin stood holding his gloves, his hat, and his cane. Kevin thought, without fondness, of the winters when he himself was a child and how his mother and father used to complain of the trouble it was to dress him to go out. His mother, after she ran away to Texas, used to send him greeting cards from Dallas, but she apparently lost track of him when he was gone to the army. His father, too, had left Bartlett, for a larger church in the Twin Cities.

Without help, W.D. shuffled through a puddle of melting ice near the back door, moving each foot an inch at a time and leaning heavily on his rubber-tipped cane. Halfway through the puddle he stopped to survey the distance he had come and, turning, he nearly lost his balance. Kevin offered his hand, but W.D. pulled his elbow away and resumed his shuffle. Where was the old man's kindness, Kevin wondered, which had been so apparent until two years ago. He never played pool anymore, never even went to the library. He read the paper with a magnifying glass, and refused to get glasses. He claimed that his eyes were as sharp as ever; it was the print that had got smaller.

Never before had W.D. found it necessary to bend himself to fit the bucket seat of a sports car. As Kevin held the door open for him, he stood there studying the seat. It was too low. If he hadn't come so far, he'd have turned back. Finally, closing his eyes, he fell into the car and dragged his cane and his legs in after him. Kevin slammed the door and hurried around to the driver's side. He started the car with a roar and set out for Rookery. Each of them, lost in thought, was silent all the way.

W.D. was thinking about his son. He'd had Sonny on his mind a lot, lately. He'd always expected to see him again, and now he had the feeling that either Sonny's time or his own was about up and if they didn't meet soon they never would. W.D. remembered the last day he saw him. It was at the County Fair in Bartlett. Viola and Sonny had sat in the backseat on their way into town, and while Viola and her mother had carried on their usual womanly conversation, Sonny had said nothing.

"You know, Ma," said Viola, "I've never seen him laugh."

"Never seen who laugh?" asked Lucille from the front seat.

"Pops."

This caused Lucille to laugh. "Oh, that's because his teeth are bad," she said.

W.D. wasn't sure his teeth were to blame, though they were repulsive to look at and had been painful by spells over the years since he had a horrible experience in a dentist's chair, a session he'd referred to ever since as "tricky." No, it was simply that he hadn't come across anything laughable in recent years. His wife and daughter were forever laughing at next to nothing. It crossed his mind that his son might be the reason he never laughed.

Walking through the shuffling, clustering crowds of the midway, W.D. noticed that Sonny kept a distance of at least five feet between himself and everybody else. There was a time or two when he seemed to have joined a group of young people in conversation, but that was only because he was their age and happened to be walking nearby. He wasn't saying anything to anybody. Then later in the evening, Lucille, W.D., and Viola, with her binoculars, climbed high into the bleachers to watch the horse show. W.D wasn't crazy about horse shows—he much preferred horseracing—but Lucille loved watching the animals trotting and cantering around the ring. W.D. was scanning the area with the binoculars when he spotted Sonny sitting on the ground, his back against a fence post, at the far and lonesome end of the fairgrounds. He was nibbling on a straw stem and thinking God knew what—long thoughts obviously, and gloomy ones as well, judging by his expression.

A couple of years earlier Sonny had taken W.D.'s second car, a junker with rusted-out floorboards, and driven to Rookery. It was a week or so before he was found and sent home. He'd been working in a bakery and sleeping in the car, and he told his mother (he hadn't spoken to his father for months) that he was glad to be home because he hated the bakery job. All he did was wash pans for the baker. He resumed his work of tending the chickens in the henhouse. He even went back to high school to finish his senior year. Lucille was overjoyed, but at commencement time Sonny didn't graduate. Lucille was devastated, and W.D. made things worse by telling her that if Sonny was not the lowest-ranking senior in the history of Bartlett High School, it was because the teachers had no device for measuring grades that low and attendance that poor.

In midsummer, after commencement, he ran away a second time. He went to Rookery again and this time bunked with his great-aunt Nancy Clancy. Nancy Clancy kept him for two nights before his behavior made him impossible to have in the apartment and she phoned W.D. and told him to come for him. He drove straight to Rookery, but Sonny had left Nancy's and it took another day for the police to find him. He was brought home looking a mess. Nancy didn't have to explain anything to W.D.—he understood how unwelcome Sonny could be—but she did anyhow. She said that on the first morning Sonny went out to look for a job, but before doing so, he finished off Nancy's bottle of blackberry brandy, which she kept in the pantry. He came home drunk before noon, and Nancy told him he had to leave. He agreed to go as soon as he caught up on his sleep, whereupon he went to bed and slept until the next morning. After he left, she found that he had been sleeping in his vomit.

As usual, Lucille was happy to have him home. It must have been motherly instinct, thought W.D., that kept her loving the boy. Surely it was motherly instinct that sent her into decline after he left the fairgrounds that night and was never seen again. The only thing that brightened her spirit was the occasional phone call from a girl named Lacey. The first time Lacey called, W.D. thought she had the wrong number, but she turned out to be Sonny's girl-friend. Neither Lucille nor W.D. had known anything about a girlfriend in their son's life. Over the phone, Lacey seemed to have the normal allotment of brains, and why, therefore, she was so helplessly in love with Sonny was be-yond W.D. She called day and night for a while, and if Lu-cille was handy he turned the phone over to her and the two of them chattered away like a couple of wrens. But if he was alone he'd answer her questions. Have you seen Sonny? "No." Have you heard from him? "No." Have you any idea where he is, because I'm worried sick. "No." W.D., since his son's disappearance, had become a man of few words, usually one word at a time. Although, by day, he was breathing easier with Sonny out of the picture, he spent as many sleepless nights as his wife, worrying about the boy because he had left without a penny to his name, and with his spirit in sad disrepair, and he was, after all, their son. It helped to have Kevin around. W.D. realized how foolish it was of him, the day Kevin showed up at the farm, to think he was Sonny. They looked nothing alike.

Kevin, driving to Rookery with W.D. silent beside him, was remembering that same day, his first full day back in Bartlett, when he wondered what he was doing there. His father no longer lived in Bartlett. He had no friends his own age. He had no work. He'd about decided to take the bus to Minneapolis and look up an army buddy who'd promised him a job in his father's lumberyard when it occurred to him that he ought to see the old man who'd befriended him through his teenage years. He drove out to the turkey farm and was met at the back door by Viola, whom he'd met one time years earlier. She ushered him into the front room. W.D., sitting in a deep chair by the window, turned to Kevin and began trembling and weeping. He put out a shaky hand and Kevin politely took it, even though his friend had grown repellently old. They didn't speak to each other. W.D. just said, "Sonny," and looked at him with tears in his eyes.

On his way out, Kevin asked Viola if he'd had a stroke.

"Not that we know of," she said. "He's just plain wore out."

A fat man then stepped out of the bedroom off the kitchen and introduced himself as Kermit Kilbride. He told his wife he'd just had a brainstorm and he asked Kevin, "How'd you like to earn yourself thirty dollars a week for just settin' on your ass?"

"Who wouldn't?"

"It's a deal. You git yourself out here bright and early New Year's morning and the job is yours." He gave Kevin a punishingly muscular handshake. "Because that's the day Viola and I are headin' south."

Viola said she'd leave their cell phone number on the kitchen counter, as well as W.D.'s medications.

Getting into his car, Kevin was struck by the possibility that the old man might be incontinent, and that the job was worth more than thirty bucks a week. He went back into the kitchen and told Kermit he couldn't do it for less than sixty.

"Sixty!" Kermit flared up in anger, but quickly relented. They settled on forty-five.

❖

KEVIN DROVE WITH a heavy foot. On the outskirts of Rookery he nearly collided with a Greyhound bus, and on a residential street he would have hit a man on a bicycle if the man hadn't steered himself into a driveway, where he tipped over in a pool of slush. Both times Kevin glanced at W.D. to assure himself that he hadn't noticed. He'd noticed, but he said nothing.

"What possessed you to think of Nancy Clancy?" he asked. "You've never been one to pay calls that I know of."

"It's March," said the old man, as if this were reason enough.

"Where does she live?"

"Damned if I know."

Kevin stopped at a gas station and found her address in a phone book. When he parked in front of the apartment building, he reached across W.D. and opened his door, then he went around and steadied him as he got to his feet.

Teetering at the curb, W.D. found himself between Kevin in his shirtsleeves and a small boy who, like himself, was bundled up for winter.

"Is this your grandpa?" asked the boy.

"No," said Kevin. As a rule, Kevin ignored children, but this one struck his fancy because he spoke so clearly for his size. He stood no higher than W.D.'s cane.

The boy walked ahead of them to the entrance of the building and asked, "Do you live here?"

"No," said Kevin.

"Who lives here?"

"Nancy Clancy."

"Who's that?"

W.D. stopped and pointed his cane at a third floor window. "She lives up there," he said, "and she's a hundred."

"A hundred years *old*?"

W.D. climbed the two steps to the heavy front door as Kevin pulled it open.

"Some turtles are a hundred," the boy said as he watched the door swing shut.

There was no elevator in the building, and Kevin, following W.D., watched his old friend pause with both feet on each step, like a pilgrim approaching a shrine. Halfway up the second flight W.D. felt giddy. A fountain seemed to be rising up his spine and bubbling in his brain, a sensation like the one he was allowed on Christmas afternoons when red wine was in good supply. He hooked his cane over his arm and gripped the banister with both hands. The fountain gradually subsided, but it sprang to life again when he took the next step. He leaned against the wall, tense and queasy. He felt as though he had outdistanced some vital part of himself— his lungs, his soul—and he was waiting for it to catch up. His right foot was asleep and he poked it with his cane.

In the narrow hallway, a scrap of paper was taped to the first door they came to, and on it was shakily printed *Mrs. N. Clancy*. Through the door came the sound of a piano, a jangling combination of treble keys that W.D. interrupted with a loud rap.

"Who is it?" called a thin voice.

"W.D." He took off his hat.

"Who?"

"W. D. Nestor. Your nephew."

The door opened and there stood Nancy, short and wrinkled and skinny as a stick, with her cheek out to be kissed. Her thick glasses were ice blue.

"Glory be," she said and then pecked him on the cheek. A faded blue dress hung down to her high black shoes and a flimsy dustcap hung over one ear.

W.D. was about to tell her she was looking younger all the time, but she seemed alert enough to know better. "You look just the same," he said.

"Of course I do. You reach a point when it's impossible to look any older."

"This is my boy, Sonny."

"How do you do, Sonny," she said, giving the young man a skeptical look. "My, how you've changed since I last saw you."

This confused Kevin. Now and then at home, W.D. had called him Sonny, but he'd thought of it as a generic term and not someone's name. He didn't think the old lady had ever seen him before. The weightless hand she offered him felt like five, cold twigs.

"Sit down, both of you. I was scrubbing my piano keys."

She snatched a rag and a can of Bon Ami off the piano stool and disappeared into her kitchen. She was quicker than W.D. remembered her.

He slowly removed his hat, gloves, and overcoat, leaving his scarf folded neatly across his chest, and lowered himself into a velvet chair by the piano. He looked for a long moment at Kevin, realizing that he was actually Charlie's Shoes and not his son. He set a crystal ashtray on his lap and rapped it with his pipe. The ashtray broke in half. Meanwhile, Kevin sat down on the piano stool and studied the ranks of fading photographs on the piano, the men choked into high, stiff collars and the ladies in plumed hats. Each face wore a serious expression and the men looked as substantial as bankers, even the young ones, but they were fading all the same.

"The surprise of my life, seeing you, Warren," said Nancy, returning with a letter in her hand and settling lightly on the center cushion of her davenport. It dipped only slightly, like a bough under a bird. She had removed her dustcap and Kevin saw that her hair, like her piano keys, had gone from white to yellow.

"It's been thirty years since you paid me a call," she said.

"Fiddlesticks. I helped you move into this apartment."

"That's not paying a call, Warren, I mean a proper call."

"Well, here I am." He picked up a brass bowl and beat it with his pipe.

When the ringing died away Nancy said, "Did you hear Gertrude passed?" He nodded. " 'Trudy,' she called herself after she moved to Oregon. Now all my nieces and nephews are dead, Warren, except you."

He had serious blockage in his pipe, and he was turning red trying to blow through the stem. "You never had much to do with Gertrude anyway," he said finally. "None of us did."

"Makes no difference. At least she was *there*. Here is her last letter to me." Nancy slipped a page out of the envelope and offered it to him, but he waved it away.

"She's buried in the West," he said.

"Glory be, is that any reason for not reading her last words? Did you leave your glasses home?"

"What glasses? I don't wear glasses." He was still busy with his pipe. "My sight is improving with age. Coming over here with the boy, I read the numbers on moving boxcars. I've never in my life needed glasses."

"Well, it's nothing to get uppity about," said Nancy. "The eyesight in your family has never been remarkable."

"Except mine. Mine is remarkable." He set his plugged pipe on the coffee table. "It was your brother Len that had the worst eyesight I ever saw short of a blind man. He tied a white handkerchief to the steering wheel of his E M F. Now don't deny it."

"My stars, why should I deny it? That was the way he drove to town and back, with the handkerchief tied to the top of the steering wheel." She turned to Kevin. "That way he could tell if he was steering straight ahead. We're talking about my brother Leonard. The road wasn't plain to him, but the handkerchief was."

"One day I was driving my Overland out north of Bartlett," said W.D., pointing into the kitchen as though Bartlett were behind the refrigerator, "and I looked around and there was Uncle Len in his E M F, coming up behind me faster than blazes. He was trying to catch up to me and he was laying a dust cloud over the land." He began to chuckle. "That was his way. Catch up behind somebody he could see and follow him into town. You know how the road used to make a jog around that big rock pile west of Bartlett? Well, I turned left to follow the road and Len lost sight of me and thought the rock pile was the back end of my Overland. He drove straight down into the ditch and up into that pile of rocks."

His laugh was silent, but it grew until it shook him like a convulsion and caused tears to spring into his eyes. Kevin had never seen W.D. laugh before. He rolled his head helplessly and bared his bad teeth. Then he squirmed around in his chair and pulled a handkerchief out of his back pocket to mop his tears.

"Wasn't it a Model A he drove into the rock pile?" said Nancy. "Or was it the Studebaker?"

"It was the E M F," said W.D., recovering. "Every Morning Fix'em."

"It's a wonder he wasn't killed that time, the poor man."

"The ditch slowed him down. It was a sandy ditch."

"But it was the E M F he died in."

"Yes, it was the E M F he died in." W.D. shook again with mirth. "He took Harold McGivern's best team with him, too. He was east of Bartlett that time. Nobody knew what he was doing east of Bartlett. His place was west. He caught sight of Harold McGivern's team and wagon and he raced down the road like blazes to catch up with it. Only trouble was—" He laughed silently, then said from behind his handkerchief, "Only trouble was Harold McGivern was coming instead of going."

Nancy folded her arms, not amused.

With a sudden, sober expression, W.D. struggled up out of the chair, the brass bowl falling from his lap.

"Where's your bathroom?"

"Through the kitchen," said Nancy, pointing.

"Harold McGivern jumped clear, but Uncle Len and the team hit head-on and tangled up and died," said W.D., shuffling into the kitchen with wet pants.

"The door by the range," Nancy called after him.

Kevin heard a phone ring in another apartment. Nancy replaced the brass bowl on the table and smoothed the doilies on the arms of the velvet chair.

"My brother Leonard," she said. "It will be sixty years ago August that he died in that accident."

"Huh," said Kevin.

"And you know, it will be fourteen years next week that Wilfred, the last of my brothers, died and I said to myself, 'Nancy, you're next. The Lord has taken the boys first and one of these days He'll be tapping you on the shoulder.' But He never did. The next thing I knew He was picking and choosing among the next generation younger than me. In fourteen years now I've seen eight nieces and nephews called, one by one, and I've been there in my black hat to see most of them blessed and buried."

"Bummer," said Kevin.

"And from the looks of Warren I expect to be in the mourners' pew at least once more. I knew the minute I opened the door and looked him in the eye. I could tell by his color."

"He's gone downhill all right."

"He's the color of chalk. And he's losing control of his bodily functions. He's my last nephew. Warren is all that's left between my generation and the one after his. He's my last bridge." Her face brightened suddenly and she sprang up from the couch and said, "Come, we'll have ourselves a cup of tea." She took the broken crystal ashtray to the kitchen, dropped it into a garbage sack, and asked Kevin to reach a high shelf for three flowered teacups.

The three of them had tea at the kitchen table. W.D. and Nancy disagreed about the date when Nancy had moved into the apartment.

"It was the fall of eighty," said W.D., "because we called on three darkies to move the piano and I gave each of them a dollar."

"The fall of eighty I was in Chicago visiting Wanda."

"It had to be the fall of eighty because you said, 'Pay the darkies and I'll pay you back' and I gave them each a dollar and you never paid me back. I've been out three dollars since the fall of eighty." He kept scooping spoons of sugar into his tea.

"We called on one colored to help with the piano, not three." Trying to speak forcefully, Nancy's voice cracked. "Back then there weren't three colored in the entire city of Rookery. And you gave him three dollars and I paid you back later in the day."

They fell silent. Nancy reached into a covered dish and drew out a prune. Kevin looked out the kitchen window. Clouds had moved over the city and it looked wintry again. A sharp breeze rippled the puddles in the alley, but they did not sparkle.

After tea, Kevin thought with great relief that the visit was over, but Nancy brought her photograph album into the kitchen and served it to her nephew like a plate of food. She carefully opened the velvet cover and pulled her chair closer as W.D. squinted at a picture in which a young man was holding a baby. They were among a group of picnickers in bonnets and suspenders.

"That was out in Uncle Leonard's pasture by the creek," said W.D. "I remember it was the day Doc Anderson went by in his Packard and it wasn't till later we heard Hilda Vanderveer had triplets. That's me there with somebody's baby. Just a youngster."

"That's not you, that's my father," said Nancy. "That baby girl is me. It shows the family twenty years before you were even born." Nancy smoothed down the tattered black page. "It's the first picture in our family ever. And I'm in it."

"That's me as a youngster, Nancy," W.D. insisted, uncurling his little finger and pressing it on the boy in the photograph. "And my brother Albert back behind there."

"Can't you understand? That baby girl is me and I'm older than you. I'm older than you, Warren, by more than a little." Nancy spit a prune pit into her palm.

"If it wasn't the day of Hilda Vanderveer's triplets, what was Doc Anderson doing going by?"

"Warren, this wasn't the day Dr. Anderson went by. You're thinking of another day. This was before Dr. Anderson ever set up practice in Bartlett."

"Who's this, then?" asked W.D., quickly turning the page. "It looks like Uncle Sherman in his overalls."

Nancy moved in for a closer look at her first husband. "That's who it is."

"See? What did I tell you? And his dog."

"Yes, our dog. Our farmhouse stands to this day on the edge of Bartlett."

On the next page they studied a photograph of W.D. in a baptismal dress. Further on they saw Leonard with one foot on the running board of his E M F. They spent a long time absorbed in the album, speaking low and sighing, like sleepers mumbling in a dream.

Dying of boredom, Kevin switched on the little radio in his shirt pocket and tuned it to a disk jockey he liked in the afternoon. He drummed on the windowsill with the tips of his fingers, and gradually gave himself up to the rhythm of a piece of rap, his foot tapping, his shoulders moving, his head bobbing.

"'S'matter with you," said W.D., glancing at him. "You got Saint Vitus' Dance?"

"The Pork Palace serves sausage six ways," announced a voice from Kevin's pocket.

"Turn that thing off," ordered W.D.

Kevin, needing noise, said, "I'll go in the other room."

In the living room, he stood looking out the window, moving his feet to the music and twirling a long, dusty tassel hanging from the drapes. He watched a man in a suit pump a bicycle down the street not quite as fast as the wind, for his necktie lay flat out in front of him as though he were being pulled by it. Caught in a tree over Kevin's car was a kite and standing under it, looking up at it, was the little boy who spoke so clearly for his size. A pickup went speeding by and splashed a sheet of icy water over Kevin's car.

"That does it," said Kevin, switching off his radio. "I'll be out front," he called to the kitchen doorway, but W.D. and Nancy paid him no attention because they seemed absorbed in the photo album.

"What a surprise to see Sonny again," said Nancy after he'd gone outside.

"Sonny, that isn't Sonny, that's Charlie's Shoes."

"I know it isn't Sonny, but you said it was."

"No, no, Charlie's Shoes, you see, is about the age Sonny was when he ran away. That's why you've got the two of them mixed up."

Deciding that it would be useless to pursue her correction, she said, "I suppose there's been no word about Sonny."

"No, no word." Although W.D. continued to look at page after page of the photo album, his mind shifted back to his incorrigible son. He'd often wondered in recent years if he was as much at fault as Lucille. Lucille always spoiled the boy of course, but maybe W.D. was too hard on him. He recalled getting out the belt now and then when Sonny was fourteen and fifteen, but it did no good. All it produced in Sonny was a hateful stare. He gave up the belt when he realized the boy was a lost cause. Sonny got to be an embarrassment. It was a shameful thing to have to hire neighbor boys to help with haying because Sonny wouldn't lift a finger. And from the time Sonny was eleven they couldn't sign up for the annual father-son dinner at church because Sonny refused to go.

W.D. felt tears welling up in his eyes, and he turned away to hide them from Nancy. He said, his voice cracking, "Sonny used to smoke marijuana. We found it in the henhouse after he left home."

❖

OUTSIDE, KEVIN SHIVERED and wished he'd worn a jacket. "Your kite's in a tree," he said to the boy standing near his car.

"My dad made it," the boy replied. He wore buckled over-shoes on the wrong feet. His face was pale and expression-less under his stocking cap.

Kevin climbed up onto the hood of his car and was able to reach the kite and bring it down. "Here's your kite," he said. "It's a good one." It was a box kite, made of fabric and thin dowels. "It must take a lot of wind to get it in the air."

"There's a lot of wind today," said the boy.

Kevin then got a rag out of his trunk and wiped his wind-shield dry, also the rest of the windows on the street side. When he finished he saw that the boy still stood there, hold-ing his kite.

"Let's try for liftoff," said Kevin, and the boy nodded, but not vigorously.

Kevin took the ball of string and led the boy out into the street and down half a block until they were out from under the trees. "Stand right there with the kite and let go when I holler," he said, paying out string until he was fifty feet away. He waited for cars to pass, then he waited for a gust of wind. "Okay!" he shouted and ran into the chilly breeze that fluttered his shirtsleeves. The kite rose a few feet, then skidded on the icy street. The boy hadn't moved from where he'd let go. Kevin motioned him forward and told him to hold the kite again. The boy obeyed. Backing across the intersec-

193

tion, Kevin payed out more string. This time as he ran, a sudden, great gust shot the kite upward and it took string faster than he could give it. He dropped the spool and let the string run out, burning his fingers. The kite rose above the bare trees, and in the stronger wind over the rooftops, it pulled like a leashed animal trying to be free.

The boy ran to Kevin, shouting, "Bring it down."

It was over the house across the street and rising higher and higher. It was like no kite Kevin had ever seen. It had none of the fragility and soaring design of ordinary kites. It looked remarkably heavy in the sky, as though something earthbound had taken flight.

"Want to hold it now?" He picked up the ball of string and offered it to the boy.

"Bring it down," the boy repeated. "My dad said not to fly it with this string. It's too weak. It will break."

"It's doing all right. Here. Take it yourself."

"Bring it down. My dad's going to buy new string on Saturday."

Kevin stopped paying out string and felt it stretch. His hands burned. The kite began behaving strangely. It turned and dipped and wrenched at the string. He gave it more string and it steadied itself.

"Bring it down," the boy begged.

Kevin glanced at him and saw that his cheeks were wet with tears. "Okay," he said, and began winding in string inches at a time. A calm settled over the neighborhood at ground level. No cars passed. Puddles lay flat as mirrors. No twig stirred. But the kite spun in the sky and the string snapped. The boy was crying aloud.

Shivering, Kevin handed him the ball of string, and switching on his radio, he hurried back to the apartment building, trotting jauntily to the music beating in his pocket. And then he saw W.D. lying on the wet grass next to the sidewalk. His cane stood upright in a snow bank nearby, his hat was in a puddle. Kevin put his arms under the old man's shoulders and raised him, but W.D. didn't help himself. He didn't hold his head up. He just scowled. Kevin asked, "Is something broke? Did you fall on the ice?" But he got no answer. Kevin then heard the ringing of a bell above his head and he turned and looked up to see Nancy Clancy reaching out under her hinged storm window, banging the brass bowl with W.D.'s pipe. Then she lowered her face to the opening and spoke inaudibly. Kevin let the old man gently down and went and stood directly under the window to catch her words. He switched off his radio.

"He's dead, I know he's dead," she said. "Looking at old pictures up here, he cried like a baby. And when he left, I came to the window to tell him he forgot his pipe, and I saw him fall. The way he fell I know he's dead. He collapsed right down."

Kevin stepped over for another look at W.D., and seeing the scowl of a dead man—the first dead person he'd ever seen—he backed away. "Call somebody," he shouted up at Nancy.

"They've been called," he heard her say as he returned to under her window. "Father Moore and 911, and I left a message on Viola's telephone. Didn't I say I'd see him dead? I no more than said it and he died. Glory be, he was my last bridge."

Looking up past Nancy's window, Kevin saw a star and

realized it was getting dark. A few snowflakes were dancing around the streetlight. "I'm coming up," he said.

"No, stay by him. He can't be lying down there all alone."

Kevin ran to pick the cane out of the snowbank and lay it beside the man. He came away quickly and repeated, "I'm coming up."

"Your place is down there until help comes." Nancy's voice was breaking and fading. "Are you a man or a boy? I've locked the door. It's no use coming up."

Two or three cars went by, then silence. Kevin's shivering became convulsive. He decided to get into his car and warm up.

Again he heard Nancy's voice. "Here's my afghan to cover him. He should be covered until help comes." She stuffed the afghan through the opening and it floated to the ground. Kevin snatched it up and wrapped himself in it. Getting into his car, he continually gunned the engine, urging warmth from the heater, and found his favorite song on the radio.

Down the block, the little boy whose kite was lost lay on a wet snowbank with his mouth open, waiting for a snowflake to fall in. He was looking up at a streetlight around which the falling snow seemed to hover like a swarm of moths. Then he heard a bell and sat up. The ringing was new to the neighborhood and after a minute he got to his feet and followed the sound across several front yards. The snowbanks he stepped in were crusty, and the grass was freezing crisp and slippery under the light, new snow. He stopped in front of the apartment building and looked up to the third floor. It was not a bell; it was an old lady extending her thin wrists out under her storm window. She was banging a brass bowl with a pipe. She dropped the bowl when she saw the boy and she put her face down to the opening.

"There he is and what did I just predict?"

To understand her, the boy had to stand directly beneath the window.

"There he is behind you," she said, and the boy turned to see a dark shape on the grass. He approached it and recognized the old man who had told him about the hundred-year-old lady. He saw his cane. His hat lay on a sheet of thin ice that had earlier been a puddle. The boy snatched at his sleeve and raised an arm, but the old man, scowling, seemed determined to stay where he was. Looking back at the old lady's window, the boy saw she still had her face to the opening and he returned to stand against the wall where he could hear her better.

"Didn't I say I'd see the poor man dead? And he wasn't anywhere near born when that picture was taken in Leonard's pasture by the creek."

Kevin, in his car, reached across the seat and opened the door and called to the boy, "Hey, get in, we'll go find your kite."

The boy left the old lady still talking and drew close to the car, then stopped. He gave Kevin a long suspicious look.

"Get in," Kevin insisted. "If we can't find it, I know a place where they sell kites. I'll buy you one. Come on."

The boy obediently crawled onto the seat next to Kevin and pulled the door shut. "Did you know there's a man lying on the ground?" he asked.

"Yeah, what a bummer," said Kevin, putting the car in

gear. He felt terrible. He knew now why he disliked old people. He hated the way they died.

The tires spun on the ice, then the car lurched away from
the curb. Snowflakes, like shooting sparks, flashed in the
headlights as he sped down the street.